IT ALL STARTED
WITH A SLIP OF THE TONGUE . . .

They both caught the slip at the same time and slapped leather as one. Moran's .45-caliber Peacemaker cleared its holster a split second sooner. Longarm's .44 Frontier, made by the same firm to fire double-action, roared a split second ahead of Moran's single-action.

A split second was all it took when the result was two hundred grains of hot lead smashing through the breastbone and into the heart. Moran fired his one and only round into the floorboards between them.

He tried to hold himself upright with his left hand gripping the bar as he died enough to let go of his smoking six-gun and collapse at Longarm's feet.

Lieutenant Grover came unstuck to gasp, "Jesus H. Christ, Buck! What was *that* all about?"

TABOR EVANS

LONGARM

AND THE HAUNTED WHOREHOUSE

JOVE BOOKS, NEW YORK

LONGARM AND THE HAUNTED WHOREHOUSE

A Jove Book / published by arrangement with
the author

PRINTING HISTORY
Jove edition / July 2002

Copyright © 2002 by Penguin Putnam Inc.

Visit our website at
www.penguinputnam.com

ISBN: 0-515-13337-X

A JOVE BOOK®
Jove Books are published by The Berkley Publishing Group,
a division of Penguin Putnam Inc.,
375 Hudson Street, New York, New York 10014.
JOVE and the "J" design
are trademarks belonging to Penguin Putnam Inc.

PRINTED IN THE UNITED STATES OF AMERICA

10 9 8 7 6 5 4 3 2 1

Chapter 1

It was on a payday night and saloons were lit up bright when a woman's scream for help rent the atmosphere of downtown Denver. So Deputy U.S. Marshal Custis Long of the Denver District Court perforce reversed his course for the Black Cat Saloon in spite of past experience.

For as all peace officers learned early on, women screamed much the same, whether inspired by pain, fear or fun. So whilst he was duty-bound to save a citizen in distress of any gender, he'd been suckered into domestic disputes before, and it sure felt silly when you had to explain how come you'd kicked the shit out of a poor old boy with a nagging wife.

Hence as he rounded the corner of an alley entrance in search of the source of the shrill sounds, Longarm, as he was better known in downtown Denver, left his .44-40 be as it rode his left hip, crossdraw, under the tails of his tobacco tweed frock coat. For the heavy-set and well-dressed gent trying to shove a kicking and screaming woman in pink organdy aboard a one-horse shay held nothing but a heap of screaming she-male in either hand as he made noises somewhere between soothing sounds and angry growls.

Neither seemed aware of Longarm until he'd strode within conversational distance to tick his hat brim to the screaming woman but address them both with, "Evening, folks. Before anyone tells me to mind my own business, I'd be the law, federal. So, no offense, I'd like to hear if this is any business of mine."

The gal in pink organdy, a henna-rinsed belle who might have looked younger without all that powder and paint on her pretty but pouty face, sobbed, "Oh, save me, kind sir! This villain is trying to abduct me for reasons too vile for words!"

The beefy gent struggling to hold on to her grunted as she caught him under the ribs with an elbow and gasped, "Bullshit! I'm only trying to take this little tramp home where she belongs, and you were right in the first place! This ain't no fucking business of your own, unless you'd care to help!"

Longarm sternly replied, "That ain't no way to talk in front of a she-male of any description, friend, and now I'd like to hear her side of the story if you don't mind."

"I mind a heap and you're about to get yourself in a whole lot of trouble, cowboy!" snapped the burly brute in black gabardine.

The young gal in organdy simmered down enough to pout, "I don't want to go home! If I wanted to be locked up in that shitty old room with only my fingers to pleasure me, I'd have never run away in the first place, so there!"

Longarm sighed and wearily addressed her abductor to ask, "Are you family or just hired by the same, you poor cuss?"

The young gal almost tore free with a sly sudden move as her bigger and stronger captor held on to grunt, "Acme Detective Agency. You don't want to know who hired me because they don't want it known a daughter of their house has been living in sin with a married man in this part of town, cowboy."

Longarm soberly replied, "I thought I told you I was the law. But I'll show you my badge and warrant if you'd care to show me a buzzer and Colorado license, garbage man."

The private detective had taken advantage of the lull in the young gal's struggles to snap a pair of handcuffs on her before she could react with a dreadful scream and an attempt to break at least one of his legs above the ankle. But, like Longarm, the burly gent was wearing stout boots under his suit pants and so her high buttons just didn't have the clout to more than hurt a lot as he freed one hand to fish under his own frock coat and take out a bill-fold. As Longarm did much the same, they were both able to flash their badges, private or federal, and when the detective allowed he'd take Longarm's badge at face value, Longarm agreed it seemed an awkward time and place, in piss-poor light, to read fine print. So as he put his own ID away Longarm asked the gal, "I know this is a delicate question, ma'am. But would you mind telling me what grade you were in the sad day Honest Abe was shot in Ford's theater?"

The girl snapped, "How should I know? I wasn't there! Are you going to save me from this brute or aid and abet him in my forced abduction?"

The detective holding her smiled for the first time to concede, "That was pretty smooth. You're the federal dick they call Longarm, ain't you? This little hussy would have lied like a rug if you'd only asked how old she was!"

Longarm sighed and said, "Thanks for warning her and saving me the effort of more trick questions. Where's this married man of which we were speaking?"

The private eye growled, warningly, "You don't really want to know. Suffice it to be said, he's seen the error of his ways and no longer means to live in sin with this wayward child."

3

"In case anybody asks," asked Longarm, "Did you kill him or scare him off?"

"Nobody is going to ask," snapped the detective, giving the gal a couple of shakes to throw her off balance before he lifted her off her feet to toss her facedown across the floorboards of the shay. This spooked the draft mare and inspired her to fight the ground anchor as the private eye clambered aboard to take a seat with one booted foot on the struggling gal's organdy-skirted rump. Then, the detective asked Longarm to hand up that anchor out of professional courtesy.

Longarm moved forward betwixt the carriage shafts and one brick wall to grasp the line and hoist the anchor improvised from a flat iron, even as he thoughtfully insisted, "I am beginning to see the light and I'm sure sorry I ain't bellied up to that bar in the Black Cat right now, pard. But, like I said, in case they ask, I got to have some names to offer the investigating officers."

The private eye insisted, "There won't be no investigation. I told you who I work for. I can tell you I am Dudly Snopes of the Acme Detective Agency. But once I deliver this snotty little snip to her legal guardians, none of this will have ever happened because the legal guardians of which I may only hint have friends in high places who ain't about to *order* investigations of events that have never taken place, see?"

Longarm allowed he was beginning to see as he tossed the ground anchor in with the kicking and cussing young gal and stepped clear of the shay. As the private eye snapped the ribbons and clucked the mare into motion down the alley, Longarm moved the other way with a shrug and renewed interest in the Black Cat Saloon or, in point of fact, a new barmaid who'd intimated, the last time Longarm had stopped by, she'd made no friends in Denver as yet and might be persuaded to go for that buggy ride he suggested if he promised to behave like a gent as

4

they parked atop Cherry Hill to admire the moonlight on the Front Range to the west.

Longarm had promised he'd pull no surprises on any lady he found himself alone with in a moonlit buggy on Cherry Hill after midnight. He doubted any lady old enough to be drawing suds in a saloon would be surprised by any moves a swain might make under such conditions. But some gals seemed to enjoy their slap-and-tickle more when they could act sort of surprised. So they liked to pretend a healthy young gent drove a healthy young woman clean the hell out to Cherry Hill after she got off work to get her views about that theory of Professor Darwin's or mayhaps how she felt about women's suffrage.

Since they only paid him half-again as much as he'd made as a top hand in his misspent youth, Longarm had been cautious about hiring a buggy for the night before quitting time at the Black Cat. But he'd reserved a surrey with leather curtains to be rolled down later, as circumstances warranted. Some women tended to doubt a gent's motives when he trimmed lamps or rolled down curtains too early in the game, bless their shy little natures.

As he strode through the batwing doors of the Black Cat, Longarm saw the boys at the bar were bellied cheek to jowl with nary a slot for a man half his size. He silently cussed that wayward gal in pink organdy as he tried to catch the eye of the harried barmaid with a starched linen apron over her maroon bodice, dashing back and forth across the duckboards behind the long zinc-topped bar as she tried in vain to keep all her customers satisfied.

A strand of her pinned-up taffy-colored hair had come loose to hang down over one big brown eye as she suddenly spotted Longarm in the press and nodded, albeit with a curious expression Longarm couldn't make out. She had no call to look so flustered by the sight of him. He'd told her he'd be by, come payday night, and by now they'd have told her he was a semiregular at the Black

5

Cat. Most gals you started up with in saloons preferred things that way.

A gal could be asking for trouble, leaving the premises with a total stranger, whilst an every-night-regular was inclined to tell tales out of school when a romance went wrong, or right enough to brag about. But like most knock-around and still-single sports, Longarm played a wider field than one neighborhood saloon after work in a metropolis the size of a state capitol. He'd long since found the free lunch counter at the handy-to-work Parthenon better than the after-hours action, whilst the Black Cat, being handy to the Union Station and so many transient hotels catering to newer gals in town, could be forgiven their stale boiled eggs and dried out sandwiches.

No adventurous traveling gal who wasn't an outright hooker would be seen unescorted in the main taproom of any Victorian saloon, of course. But like most of its kind, the Black Cat provided "family rooms" off to one side where more properly brung-up ladies and gents could set at bitty tables pretending they were there to meet someone they'd already been introduced to. So, once his intended lady of the evening brushed by without catching Longarm's eye again he shrugged and drifted through the smoke-filled taproom to enter a less crowded but way smaller chamber, where a half dozen women of all sizes and shapes were singing "Lorena" with twice as many men of mixed description.

Knowing the form, Longarm took a seat in one corner after he'd ticked his hat brim to the fat gal seated at that particular bitty table and been rewarded with an indifferent nod. She didn't seem to know the words of the song but turned from him as if to learn them as he considered joining in, decided not to, and just waited quietly until a male waiter who'd been watching the door came in as expected to take his order.

Raising his voice a tad to cut through the wails of the

sad old song about poor "Lorena," Longarm allowed he'd like a jigger of Maryland rye with a scuttle of draft to chase it. The waiter dryly remarked that seemed a heap of beer to chase a tad of whisky, but since Longarm had observed the courtesy of ordering at least *some* serious liquor in a family room, he didn't argue. He turned to the fat gal as he asked Longarm, instead, what the lady was having.

Longarm had already noticed there was nothing on the table between them. As the fat gal turned with a sticken look, Longarm asked their waiter to fetch her a gin and tonic, seeing it was such a warm night, and put one knee against hers, under the table, to warn her not to put a foot in his mouth.

She did, of course, bleating, "Wait! We're not together!" as the waiter turned away to fill the order without looking back. Waiters in the Black Cat were paid to keep the liquor flowing, not to ask possibly confused drunks what on earth they were talking about.

Edging away from Longarm the fat gal protested, "How dare you presume so upon an honest working girl alone in this great city, sir? I assure you that if I were the sort of woman who drank gin, I could well afford to buy my own!"

He decided she might not be bad looking if she'd lose no more'n twenty pounds as she continued, pink lips all aquiver, "Had I wanted anything at all at this hour, I assure you I could have had room service deliver it to my suite at the Palace Hotel!"

Longarm eased back to reassure her as he soberly replied, "That may be true, ma'am. But if you aim to kill a few late hours in this family room whilst they make up your quarters at the Palace, you're expected to order drinks now and again."

Before she could answer, their waiter came back with the smaller glasses and a big scuttle of suds on a tray. As

7

he set them down Longarm snapped a silver cartwheel down on the tray to add that the two of them would like some ham and cheese sandwiches along with a couple of bowls of chile con carne with oyster crackers, too.

As the waiter left a second time, the crowd had switched to "Red River Valley" and the fat gal was trying to hide her face in her kerchief as she commenced to whimper like a lost child.

So Longarm reached out to pat the back of one plump hand as he soothed, "Don't cry. It's going to be all right. How long has it been since you found yourself stranded out this way?"

Chapter 2

She tried to snub him dead 'til that waiter came back with the stale sandwiches and fresh-made chili con carne, steaming like a Mexican lava flow, before the healthy appetite she'd been blessed or cursed with betrayed her resolve and forced her to allow she'd try just a bite, to be polite.

As she dug in to make Longarm suspect she hadn't eaten all day, she confided they called her Kitty. So Longarm told her who he was and by the time she'd put away all her chili and half his ham on rye, Longarm was starting to feel left out. For it appeared he was the only white man west of the Big Muddy who hadn't used and abused poor Kitty since she'd left her good home and kind parents to seek her fortune in the golden West. Longarm had been raised too polite by his own kind parents to let on he'd heard her tale of woe before, many, many times. For some men would do or say most anything to have their way with an innocent young thing and some young things kept falling for the same old bullshit long after one might think they'd gotten over feeling innocent.

In sum, she'd confided by the time she'd washed down the last of the oyster crackers with beer—that gin and

9

tonic having vanished like the snows of yesteryear with her chili con carne—some sweet-talking rascal she'd met in Saint Lou had promised her cucumbers and other wonders if only she'd share his Pullman compartment out to Denver, where he was very big in butter and eggs. Only that had been days ago and her money had run out, waiting for him to rejoin her at that hotel across from the Union Station. She looked wounded as she confided the hotel was holding her traveling bags whilst she waited, she'd told them, for that money order from home.

Longarm refilled both their glasses as he tallied the likely cash totals in his head, warning himself not to be a sucker. For next payday lay a month ahead and that run of luck he'd had at the card house the other night had likely been a fluke.

He asked Kitty what she did for a living when she wasn't running off to strange towns with slick-talking strangers. She said she'd been a shop girl back in Saint Lou, bored, bored, bored and dying for a little romance and adventure as the cobwebs of spinsterhood seemed ever thicker with each lonely passing weekend. He didn't really want to hear about the slick-talking customer who'd come by to buy this, that and the other as he'd painted pretty pictures of western sunsets from the veranda of his big Rocky Mountain spread until one thing had led to another and she didn't have a job in Saint Lou anymore.

Longarm tallied, even as a still small voice of reason insisted from a mental corner that anybody who *sounded* as dumb as this one might be a slicker-than-average fibber. Then he decided the Lord might have had emergencies such as this one in mind when he'd dealt such great hands in that card house, all evening, the other night. So he told his common sense to just hush before he turned to Kitty to confide, "I got this horse and buggy on ice at the livery across the way. Along about midnight I plan to drive out to Cherry Hill with another lady."

The not-too-bad but way-fatter Kitty sniffed, allowed it was a free country, and asked why she should care about his private life.

He said, "That's as much about this other lady as you're ever going to hear, no matter how things turn out, Miss Kitty. I only wanted to assure you I ain't a moon calf lusting for your fair white body and out to lead you astray with more false promises, see?"

She said, "No. I have no idea what you're talking about."

So he said, "I had a run of luck the other night, and I just got paid this afternoon. So I'm feeling flush and, thanks to times my luck didn't run so good, I know how it feels to feel busted. Right now you're feeling sick and sort of empty no matter how much you may eat at a given moment and . . . Aw, for Pete's sake, don't blubber up like that, Miss Kitty. I'm trying to tell you how we're going to make it all better!"

She sobbed, "How? I'm like that wayfaring stranger in that sad old song, a long way from home in the gathering dusk with nobody to turn to!"

He nodded soberly and said, "I noticed. I've been down that road, Miss Kitty. So here's what we're going to do. I'm going to, ah, lend you enough to bail you out and head you back to Saint Lou with say a few days' worth of eating money to last you 'til you get that job or a better one back. For openers, how much do you owe that hotel?"

Others in the family room had lost interest in the "Red River Valley" as Kitty wailed, "Oh, heavens, you can't mean that! I owe them for three days, at double rates plus at least five dollars room service!"

He nodded and said, "*Bueno*. Twenty bucks should bail you out at the hotel and get you back to Saint Lou if you don't mind sitting up all the way. Another five, or let's say ten ought to keep you from wasting away to nothing before you can get another job. So what say I lay out one

11

month's day labor and I'll expect you to pay me back two dollars a month for six months, by mail, once you get settled in back to Saint Lou?"

A thinner-but-uglier young gal at the next table trilled, "Take it, Honey! I wish somebody would offer *me* thirty dollars for doing nothing just once in my own life!"

Everybody laughed. Kitty flushed darkly and declared they'd been trying to hold a private conversation. So the ugly gal suggested they sing "Row Row Row Your Boat" and they began. The regulars were friendly at the Black Cat, most nights.

So the deal was done, even as Kitty flustered and protested as Longarm pressed an eagle and a double-eagle in gold across the table at her under his considerable palm. She'd just demurely made the money disappear when the taffy-headed barmaid he'd set his sights on came in with an order for another table. She pretended to stop by their table on her way out and bend over to ask if they needed anything.

Longarm confided, "This is Miss Kitty from Saint Lou and before she leaves for the station she might be able to use some black coffee, Miss Barbara."

The taffy-haired Barbara said she'd have the regular waiter fetch the coffee and then, hesitating as if to make certain everyone else in the room was rowing their boats too loudly for her to be overheard, she bent lower to confide, "I won't be able to meet you after work, Custis. Something, ah, came up."

Longarm asked how she felt about any night later in the coming week, and when Barbara said she'd be . . . too busy, Longarm smiled thinly and allowed he understood.

After she'd left, blushing like a rose, Longarm chuckled and told the unlucky lover at his table, "I sure hope, for Barbara's sake, that something that came up really means it. She's a good old gal and I'd hate to see her give up this job and run off to Saint Lou with some slick-talking rascal."

Kitty stared owlishly at him to marvel, "You suspect she's going out with some other man and you're not *angry*, ah, Custis?"

He shrugged and said, "Fair is fair and when a man don't have butter and eggs or castles in the sky to offer, he can't blame a lady if she makes a more practical choice. I suspicion I might do better with you ladies if I lied some about my current job and possible future. But it ain't no fun to cheat at checkers, neither."

He raised his glass to add, "So here's to Miss Barbara and a better man or bigger liar, and let's say no more about what might have been, out to Cherry Hill by moonlight."

The plainer gal a table over had been listening in under all that boat rowing. She slid closer to urge Kitty to, "Offer to ride out to Cherry Hill with him, honey! A girl can go home to Saint Lou any old time and none of us are getting any younger!"

Kitty blushed and insisted she wasn't that sort of a gal. Longarm smiled friendly but firm as he told the well-meaning young thing with the unfortunate nose that they were trying to have them a private conversation. So she sniffed they were both conversing dumb and slid the other way to join the sudsy singing in a family room where nobody seemed related to anyone else.

Kitty made Longarm write down his address on a page torn from his field notebook and put it away with the money he'd "loaned" her as they both rose from the table. She said he didn't have to carry her back to her hotel. When he walked her out the side entrance, demuring, she insisted, "Really, it's best I return alone in case . . . I mean, so nobody at my hotel will wonder about . . . us."

Longarm nodded understandingly but said, "He ain't going to be there, Miss Kitty. But have it your own way and far be it for me to cause a scandal in the lobby of a transient hotel."

Oblivious or unaware of the sarcasm, the pretty-faced fat gal stood tippy-toe to peck him on one cheek before she turned with a sob to literally run for it down the alley toward the cross street to her hotel near the station. Longarm knew it wasn't far. So what the hell, it was a free country.

Standing alone with his back to the side entrance to the Black Cat, Longarm fished out a three-for-a-nickel cheroot as he muttered to himself, aloud, "I keep telling you to quit tilting at windmills, Don Quixote, but will you ever listen? What in blue blazes did you do with a month's day wages, just now?"

A she-male voice from the gloom of the alley behind him softly told him, "I thought it was lovely. I was sure you were going to talk her into that buggy ride and we both knew she'd have gone along with the notion if you'd insisted. But to my pleased surprise you seem to be no more than a nice gent who meant just what you'd said, inside!"

Longarm wearily turned, his cheroot unlit as yet, to smile sheepishly down at that ugly gal from inside. He didn't ask how come she'd followed them outside. They'd already established she was nosey in more ways than one. Those big blue eyes to either side of her enormous nose were friendly as well as worldly. So he laughed and confessed, "All three of us knew I could have taken advantage of a not-too-bright gal who'd grown used to being taken advantage of. But have you ever been forced to sit through that tedious opera about *La Traviata* by Mr. Verdi, Miss . . . ah?"

"Cecilia, Cecilia Mandalian," she replied, moving closer to ask him what a Verdi opera might have to do with what had just transpired.

Putting the unsmoked cheroot away, Longarm sug-

14

gested they talk about it back inside, or anywheres else she might desire. So Cecilia said her own place was nearby, she'd had enough to drink, and suggested he offer his views on *La Traviata* over coffee and cake.

So they soon wound up in her kitchen above the hardware Cecilia owned and ran on Curtis Street when she wasn't rowing her boat at the Black Cat. As she scrambled some eggs to go with the pickled grape leaves stuffed with Lord-only-knew-what, she explained how she had reverted to her Armenian family name after her hardware-dealing husband of the Scotch-Irish persuasion had died of a heart stroke after unloading a ton of bob wire on a hot summer day. She explained, and he felt no call to argue, that a face like hers took heaps of explaining when offered alongside a name such as Maguire. As Longarm watched her bustle about in her summerweight rainy-susan skirts and tight bodice, both a shade of aquamarine that set off her eyes and blue-black hair sort of nice, he decided the figure under the well-chosen summer outfit more than made up for a friendly eagle-beak and a jaw-bone too small by a half for the rest of her. She poured his coffee first and as she rustled up the rest, Longarm morosely related the sad tale of *La Traviata*.

He explained, "The worse part, for me, was being dragooned into escorting a Denver society gal to her blamed private box at the blamed Denver Opera House on a night they were showing off such an awful opera!"

As she bustled he considered and conceded, "Some of the *tunes* of La Traviata weren't bad and both the tenor and the fat lady singing the part of the dying . . . naughty gal, were both in fine voice. *La Traviata* means 'naughty gal' in Eye-talian, I was given to understand, and she seemed all of that, selling her favors to barons and such, whilst stealing a married man from his wife and children whilst, all the time, through one aria after another, she was dying of consumption."

He chuckled wryly down at his coffee cup to observe, "The lady I'd escorted to the opera kept poking me in the ribs for laughing about a soprano of some two hundred pounds or more wasting away to nothing as she kept insisting that was happening, song after song after song."

Cecilia joined him at the table with the handsome late-night spread she'd prepared, asking once again what a fat opera singer had to do with the fat shop girl they'd just sent back to Saint Lou.

He didn't recall anybody else chipping in, but life was too short to waste time arguing with a woman, so he said, "The pair of 'em being fat wasn't what made the opera so tedious. What made *La Traviata* so tedious was that from scene 1, act 1 everybody on stage or in the audience *knows* how it's all fixing to pan out in the end, with all the tunesome songs and childishly stupid lyrics as the dying fat lady wastes away all over the stage."

Cecilia allowed she wasn't familiar with the plot of *La Taviata*.

Longarm washed down some stuffed grape leaf, deciding it had been stuffed with fried rice and chopped olives, before he told such a swell cook, "The tale of *La Traviata* ain't complicated as say *Little Red Riding Hood*. As she first appears on stage, she's throwing a wild party at her Paris parlor house for other high-priced hookers and their well-heeled johns. You find out in that first scene that she's just come home from a consumption sanatorium and she's tottering about the stage looking decidedly unwell. So anyone with even one lick of sense knows she's fixing to kick the bucket, soon, unless she cuts down on her wild ways. But she won't, or can't, and when this foolish married-up man from the south of France wants to leave his family and move in with her, she lets him. So how would you say a lust-affair as dumb as that one has to turn out?"

Cecilia shrugged—she had nice shoulders—and decided, "Not too well, and what could they have possibly seen in one another? I mean, with him a blithering idiot and her . . . in poor health?"

Longarm grimaced and continued, "He kisses her all over the stage as she collapses like a deflating balloon, over and over and over until at last she dies, a lot, singing all the while about what a rotten break fate dealt her, after a totally selfish life of pleasure for fun and profit. When I asked the lady in the opera box with me why the fat gal on stage rated an egg in her beer, I was told I had no soul. But it seemed to me that even if you could feel sorry for a real hooker with a bad case of the consumption, there was no *story* to that opera about the same. I mean, there wasn't one *surprise* to the whole show. Everything turned out exactly as you'd *expect* such things to turn out, if you see what I mean."

Cecilia rose from the table, softly saying, "I see what you mean. I was listening when you told that silly fat girl there was no fun in cheating at checkers because that way there was never a *surprise!*"

There was no delicate way to say he'd seen exactly how things of a country nature were bound to turn out with a born loser running to lard. So he said nothing as the blue-eyed Armenian gal stepped out of her kitchen by way of a beaded curtain, trilling back, "Oh, fess up, now, Custis. You can't say everything this evening has gone exactly according to plan, up to now."

Longarm chuckled wryly and confessed, "Well, I never expected to meet up with either of you other ladies after being left in the lurch by my . . . chosen target. So I reckon you could say things have turned out at least a mite surprising."

Then his jaw dropped as Cecilia Mandalian reappeared in the doorway to part the beaded curtain, smiling down at him naked as a jay and built so fine it hurt to look at her with pants on!

So he took his pants and everything else off as she coyly retreated into the darkness beyond, promising other surprises to follow, and he had to allow it felt surprising as all get-out to have a gal with a nose like that go down on him without one word of warning.

Chapter 3

It wasn't easy. But after she'd surprised him some other ways, Longarm finally got them going at it the old-fashioned way with a pillow under her rollicking rump and her ankles locked across the nape of his neck. It felt surprising just to kiss a gal with such odd facial features, although her firm, shapely body seemed flawless as well as mighty flexible from the chin down. When she suggested another position before they came in that one, Longarm allowed he was doing just fine where he was and touched bottom to prove it as he made her gleep in mingled pain and pleasure.

She begged him not to look at her when he struck a match to light their second-wind cheroot. So he didn't, having memorized the wonders of her solid curves by braille as well as that fleeting glance she'd offered him earlier by lamplight from the kitchen.

As she commenced to fiddle with his privates before they'd half smoked the skinny cheroot, Longarm asked how come they couldn't just sort of float down the river in the moonlight, seeing the night, as well as the two of them, were still young.

She sighed sort of bitter and allowed she felt she had

to prove herself in bed to make up for her ugly face and added, "It's not often I find myself in bed with a man I can trust. So I have to make his sacrifice worth his while, don't I?"

He soberly replied, "I'd be insulting your store-keeping brains if I said you were pretty as Miss Ellen Terry or the Princess of Wales, Miss Cecilia. But I'd hardly call making love to anyone built like you a *sacrifice*! Run that part about trusting men past me some more. What are you afraid of? No offense, but it was your suggestion I come in your mouth, as I recall."

She half sobbed she wasn't worried about where men might come in or about her, as long as she could trust them not to pester her with proposals of marriage.

Longarm soberly assured her he'd never insult her by asking her to marry up with him.

She said, "I knew that, back at the Black Cat. You've never noticed me among the less attractive regulars, Custis. But I've been told a heap about you and I know who the society woman you escort to that private opera box might be, too."

He quietly but firmly suggested they leave possible identities up in the clouds and assured her nobody would ever hear it from him that she liked to swallow.

She sighed and said, "I knew you never kissed and told when I told that silly fat girl to get in that buggy with you, Custis! But now that she's blown her own chance for a night with the famous Longarm, I don't mind saying I'm glad it was me, in spite of your disappointment."

Longarm snorted smoke out both nostrils and snapped, "There you go insulting us both again, Miss Cecilia. Can't you see that had I wanted to spend the night with that other gal I'd have *spent* the night with that other gal?"

Cecilia let out a triumphant laugh they'd have heard downstairs had her hardware been open and chortled, "I *thought* you might have been putting on that big brother act to assure me you weren't after anything but pussy! Fess up! You'd heard from the other regulars about that fortune-hunting Armenian salesman I'd had so much trouble getting rid of and you wanted to let me know money didn't mean that much to you, right?"

"Well, something like that," Longarm conceded, knowing she wanted him to, even though he had no idea what she was talking about. So that flattered her so much she came close to throwing his back out as they went at it hot and heavy to wind up on the rug, that time, with her on top, trying to cossack dance without letting his old organ grinder get away from her gyrating ring-dang-doo.

So a right surprising time was had by all, and, as they smoked some more, he began to understand her confused emotions better and suspect he understood why she'd had so much trouble with other men in spite of being such a great lay.

She surprised him some more as he learned she was considered ugly by Armenian standards, not because of her heroic nose, but because of those big blue eyes he'd found prettier than the rest of her face. It seemed her own mother had been ashamed to bear a blue-eyed baby that might or might not be its nominal father's child but certainly had two—not one—but *two* evil eyes! When Longarm asked how her elders had come up with such an odd notion, Cecilia assured him Greeks and Turks as well as Armenians all agreed blue eyes were evil and unnatural, even though they couldn't agree on less important matters such as the name of the Lord or what day Easter fell on. It was just as well he didn't have to explain his amused expression in the dark as she told him there were still villages back in her old country where a blue-eyed stranger could be stoned to death as a devil.

Taking his thoughtful silence as a need for reassurance, she kissed his bare shoulder and told him gray eyes like his own were just considered ugly by country folk out

21

Armenia way. She'd known that one Armenian salesman who'd asked her to marry had lied like a rug when he'd assured her he didn't believe her true blue eyes were all that evil. Longarm felt no call to ask if the gent in question had wound up on the rug with such an athletic little thing. He didn't want to know, and it seemed possible any gent proposing to the sole owner of a hardware on Curtis Street might decide he'd found his fortune at long last.

It was just as possible, albeit he was too polite, and too wise in the ways of the womanly mind to say it, that a quick-witted hardware-pushing gal who'd been pushed around by a fickle fate had commenced to make self-fulfilling predictions about simply horny cusses she'd sort of surprised with her odd approach to romance.

Those head doctors over to Vienna town had big words for the ways men and women both fucked up their love lives by sticking their own hopes and fears in the minds of others. Having been assured by old-country elders her beautiful blue eyes were ugly, the poor old gal never worried about her dreadful nose or weak chin as she avoided the gaze of the superstitious and, having wound up with a business beyond the dreams of Middle Eastern peasantry, she felt certain men headed west to seek their fortunes panning for gold or breeding stock were anxious to sign away their freedom just to peddle hardware out Colorado way.

She assumed, without asking, that a man snuffing out a spent smoke was anxious for another blow job, or wanted to shove it to her Greek when he only had dog-style in mind. But at least they were facing a slugabed Sabbath morn, once he satisfied her hungry little love-maw, and he had to admit few Saturday nights turned out as unusual.

Letting his mind wander with her on top again, Longarm felt sure that by then neither the fat waif he'd sent home to Saint Lou nor even the taffy-haired temptress he'd been after to begin with would have still been awake and screwing like a mink in season. He'd known all too well, before he'd sent Kitty on her way, how the not so-bad-looking but unpleasingly plump shop girl would cry when she came, then beg to shack up with him forever and a day.

He suspected the taffy-headed Barbara might have given him a finer ride without letting him know for certain whether she'd come or not. Fickle-hearted gals who sized men up for their pocket jingle instead of anything else in their pants suffered delusions of desirability out of all proportion to anything they really had to offer any man. So he decided he'd drawn the best cards dealt at the Black Cat that particular evening when he rolled the hot natured Cecilia on her shapely back to finish right, to her passionate delight.

Then they got four hours sleep or less before she woke him up for a morning quickie while it was still dark out and served him a swell breakfast in bed as a neighborhood rooster was suggesting everybody else ought to wake up. You knew how fashionable a part of town you were in, along about that hour of the morning, because east of Lincoln Street you were no longer allowed to keep chickens out back, lest you disturb the well-earned rest of richer folk.

As they et in bed Cecilia droned on about her earlier rare and not-too-successful love affairs. Longarm failed to see why so many women tended to subject a new initiate to that hazing. If her intent was to have him assure her he'd never do this or that to any woman, the way those other brutes had, he'd learned the hard way it was best to just agree most men were brutes and make no promises one might regret with one's pants on. He had no call, since he knew she didn't want to be told that she was commencing to get on *his* nerves with her . . . *intensity* was likely the best description for it.

23

Just as men who tried too hard to be the life of every party and the corpse at every wake wound up alone at home and uninvited more often than not, women with dramatic personalities and overly romantic natures were inclined to drain a man of six week's worth of passion in a night and wishing she'd for Chrissake shut up for just a cotton-picking minute. But Longarm tried to be a good sport as she jawed at him all through an otherwise swell breakfast. For her bare tits still looked grand in the dawn light sneaking past the drawn blinds of her bedroom. So a lazy Sunday and, hell, maybe one more night with such a good cook and great lay might not have been too great a burden for a natural man to bear.

But then she put him to work. Downstairs, in her closed and shuttered hardware, helping her "rearrange" her stock. That was what she called the two of them shifting hundred-pound nail kegs or halfway assembled Aermotor Brand windmills from one spot on the sawdust coated floorboards to another—"rearranging."

Things might have been worse. Thanks to the place being closed for the day and shuttered from public view along Curtis Street, they got to work naked as jays by the dim light and every once in a while, at times less surprising folk might have stopped for a breather, Cecilia begged to be ravaged some more atop a counter or across a barrel. But she forbade him to smoke, lest he set the place on fire, and by the time she hauled him back upstairs for a swell noon dinner, Longarm was sure that shortly after the first cavewoman dragged the first caveman into her cave by his hair, she'd doubtless decided *that* rock would go better on *this* side of the cave if he'd be good enough to muscle *this* rock over to *that* side. For after all his sweat and screwing down below, he'd have been whipped with snakes before he could have seen any improvement at all.

So after having her across the kitchen table for dessert,

Longarm regretfully told Cecilia he had to wash, dress and get going, out to the Diamond K to investigate suspicious brands.

As he'd hoped, the hardware dealing widow woman knew and cared as much about branding stock as most women. So she bought his lie, or said she did, and let him off with a last passionate kiss and his promise to return for more, though hell might bar the way, as soon as he might be able.

Then Longarm trudged west to Larimer Street, crossed the Cherry Creek bridge to the south, and made it home to his furnished digs in an even less fashionable neighborhood, walking sort of funny.

He went upstairs to strip and flop facedown across a bedstead he'd found lonely on many an earlier occasion. But, Jesus H. Christ, it felt so good to just shut one's eyes with the certain knowledge nobody was going to wake one up with one's cock in a woman's mouth before one was damn-well ready to be woke up some more!

As he let his big overstimulated frame melt into the crisp fresh bedding, Longarm's memories drifted back to that secret vice he'd hidden from the others back in his army days, doubting other kids his age at the time might understand how swell it felt, after weeks or months in action or even on garrison duty, to go on leave in some quiet town behind the lines and check into a hotel, enjoy a hot bath and warm restaurant meal, and just turn in, alone, propped up against crisp linen pillows in a soft feather bed with a good book to read by the light of a lamp one got to trim when and if one damn well wanted it trimmed, to sleep or not to sleep as one chose, with nobody snoring or jerking off in the bunk above one, for as late the next morn as one damn well pleased. So an average three-day pass allowed plenty of time for wine, women or song to follow, once a soldier boy had turned his fool self back into a human being for the time left.

But, of course, not even the session Cecilia had put him through could inspire more than twelve hours rest for such an active frame as Longarm's. So he was, damnit, wide awake before cock-crow on Monday morning, and enjoying a leisurely breakfast of fried eggs over a T-bone smothered with chili con carne before sunrise.

Not wanting to set a dangerous precedent, Longarm killed some time with the penny slot machines in the Larimer Street arcade, gracefully declined the three-ways-for-one-dollar offer of a not-bad looking *desperada* and shopped for fresh smokes along the way before he showed up for work at the federal building unusually early.

Naturally. to his relief, Longarm saw nobody got to work there any earlier than his boss, Marshal Billy Vail, or the brownnosing Henry who played the typewriter out front.

Longarm's conscience was clear as he ambled in a few minutes before their office was officiously open for the day. So he failed to see why Henry shot him that teacher's pet now-you're-gonna-get-it! look as he motioned with his prissy head to say, out loud, "You're wanted bad in the chief's office, Deputy Long."

So, still clear of conscience, Longarm ambled on back, lighting a new three-for-a-nickel smoke in self-defense to find, as expected on opening the door, the inner chambers of Marshal William Vail of the Denver District Court enshrouded ceiling to floor in the pungent blue haze given off by old Billy's expensive but dreadful cigars.

Leaving the door open so's some smoke might escape, Longarm made his way to the one and only guest chair on the public side of Vail's cluttered desk to sink down uninvited and ask, "You told Henry you wanted to see me, boss?"

The somewhat older and way shorter and stouter lawman on the far side of all that stinky smoke snapped, "You're damned A, you total asshole! This time you've really torn it! Don't you have any sense at all when it comes to *women*, you romantic-natured fool? What in Gawd's name ever possessed you to mess with all that trouble in skirts Saturday night?"

Chapter 4

It wasn't easy. But Longarm managed not to ask, "Which one?" as Billy Vail went on glaring at him through the thinning smoke whilst the banjo clock on one oak-paneled wall tolled seven times. Longarm knew he hadn't done shit to Barbara or Kitty the other night, whilst Cecilia made no sense. For they'd parted friendly after she'd thanked him profuse for the best reaming out of her old ring-dang-doo she'd enjoyed in ages.

Since Longarm declined to own up to his sins, Billy Vail growled, "For Gawd's sake, she's barely fifteen and her daddy plays poker with Governor Pitkin and Silver Dollar Tabor!"

To which Longarm could only reply, "That well may be, but you have my word as an enlisted man I have not been fooling with any fifteen-year-old pussy unless a gal who assured me she was a widow woman of some means was lying like hell!"

Vail insisted, "Do you deny you interfered last Saturday night when a responsible adult was attempting to rescue an underaged runaway from living in sin with a married man?"

Longarm heaved a sigh of relief and replied, "Oh, *her*?

I'd clean forgot an alley interval with a private detective and a henna-rinsed sass who needed her mouth washed out with laundry soap. It was no big deal, boss. I only asked what all the screaming was about. He showed me his buzzer and I could see she was too young to be running loose in that part of town at such an hour. So we parted friendly and we each went his own way and that was all there was to the minor breach of the peace that evening."

Vail shook his balding head to say, "No it wasn't. The teenaged adultress rescued from a life of shame was Miss Susan Hawker, the one and only spoiled rotten child of the smelter-owning Hawkers of Central City, Black Hawk, Leadville and other points of interest all along the nearby Rockies. It's my unofficious understanding they paid a heap to have her rescued by that Acme Agency lest one word of their family scandal appear on officious public records."

Longarm shrugged, flicked tobacco ash on the office rug in hopes of keeping down the carpet mites, and asked, "So how come you just clouded up and rained all over me, then? Like I told you, that private eye had picked her up and seemed in control of the little sass when we parted friendly. I had nothing to do with her recapture. I can't even say where she'd been shacked up, or with whom."

Vail grimaced and said, "I've told my own pals in high places to point that out to her family. Their worry is that you *know* she was shacked up with a married man and, worse yet, you *saw* her handcuffed and red-eyed, like a common street walker getting rounded up for lewd public behavior. Did I mention how the smelting Hawkers shun public mention of their family affairs? They're New Englanders who hold a woman's name must only appear in print when she's born, when she marries and when she dies. Period and never another whisper of her name in public!"

Longarm nodded and said, "I've met the type. One who shall be as nameless makes me sneak out her back door before daybreak. But as I have assured her, too, I hardly ever brag to the *Police Gazette* about my love life. Could any rich snob be dumb enough to suspect I'd pass on idle gossip to the *Rocky Mountain News*, even if any paper they no doubt advertise with would *print* unwholesome rumors I could offer no way to prove?"

Vail replied, "It seems they'd rather feel safe than sorry and, damn it, Custis, when are you going to stop flicking them fucking ashes on my fucking rug?"

"When you set up a fucking ashtray on this side of that fucking desk," Longarm replied with a weary sigh, adding, "Can we get back to them fucking smelter owners with a daughter too young for a married-up man to be fucking? I just told you all I know about her."

Vail said, "You know too much. I'm being pressured to transfer you to another federal district. They don't choose to believe I just don't have such powers. I told them I could fire you with a letter commending you to say Fort Smith or Sacramento, leaving you mighty pissed off and even more likely to go to papers they *don't* advertise in with a tale of injustice and whitewash. But, like I just said, they're all hot and bothered about that hellcat on their hands so, all in all, I reckon this would be as fine a time as any to have you tidy up some pesky federal business out in the Four Corners County."

Longarm knew better than to point out what a piss-poor time it was to visit the canyon lands where the corners of the uncertainsomely charted Arizona, Colorado, New Mexico and Utah borders crossed at right angles in the middle of nowheres much. Longarm knew his boss knew the empty semiarid Colorad Plateau got long stretches of not enough rain mixed with late summer gullywashers of biblical flash flooding, with the calendar reading August at the moment. So Longarm just flicked more ash and finally Billy Vail admitted, "We've been asked by the Bureau of Indian Affairs to ride herd on a team of health workers, anxious to vaccinate a lost tribe rumored to be holding out in some uncharted canyon betwixt Fort Defiance and Canyon de Chelly. So, seeing you know that country better than anyone else we got, now that Kit Carson is no longer with us . . ."

"Bullshit!" Longarm cut in, adding, "No white man or honest Indian can say he knows beans about a tableland of ancient sea-bottom way bigger than Ireland, thrust a mile above present sea level and crazy quilted with countless unsurveyed canyons. What sort of Indians are they missing over yonder, and why can't the B.I.A. just let them be if they ain't bothering anybody?"

Vail patiently replied, "Some day, after you've worked for the government as long as me, you'll understand how it bothers political appointees to just leave people be. Our progressive Secretary Schurz of the Interior has decreed all Indian wards of the government should be and therefore *must* be vaccinated against the smallpox. So when the South Ute Agency this side of Fort Defiance got word of unregistered and hence unvaccinated holdouts up some uncharted canyon somewheres betwixt the Hopi, Navaho and Ute, a team of do-gooders was assembled back East to head out our way and civilize the redskinned sons of bitches.

"As we speak, they're fixing to arrive by broad guage. You'll join up with 'em here and travel far as Durango by D & RGRR narrow guage before you'll be called upon to get serious. We both know there ain't nothing more civilized than pack train trails from Durango down to Fort Defiance and, like I said, our B.I.A. health workers will be eastern dudes who may need nursemaiding in the Four Corners Country. That'll give me the excuse to assign you to field duty, and since none of them B.I.A. dudes will have met you before, I might as well introduce you

32

as that Crawford cuss you assume yourself to be whilst working undercover now and again. How come you like to be known as Custis Crawford, undercover, Custis Long?"

Longarm smiled thinly and confided, "Inside joke. Crawford Long was the sawbones who invented painless surgery just in time for that war they invited me to in my teens. After that, Reporter Crawford of the *Denver Post* refuses to listen when I ask him to stop making me out so heroic in those newspaper yarns. So, as I've warned the chubby cuss, it'll serve him right when reporters of the future record the furious frontier exploits of some mysterious cuss called Crawford."

He took another drag on his cheroot and asked, "How come you want me sneaking up on sneaky Indians undercover, boss? Are they supposed to be expecting visitors? If so, how come you're only sending me and not an army column down yonder with those B.I.A. dudes?"

Vail made a wry face and confided, "The War Department wants no part in the expedition. Fort Defiance is under-strength, and sensitive as it is about the Indians, they know of laughing at 'em. As you hardly need to be told, the Four Corners country can be rough on greenhorns; most of our experienced troopers are down along the border this summer because of that Apache scare, and it ain't true that Mister Lo, the poor Indian, has no sense of humor. Fort Defiance reports that when they've asked about that lost tribe of Chindi down by Canyon de Chelly, the Indians just snicker and say sardonic things in their own mysterious lingo."

Longarm nodded, then frowned through the blue haze to demand, "Did you just say that B.I.A. team is on its way west to vaccinate a lost tribe of *Chindi*?"

When Vail allowed he thought that was the way they'd spelled it out, Longarm laughed like hell and said, "Somebody in Washington has been sold a map to the Seven

Cities of Cibola! Don't you know what a *chindi* is, in the Diné dialect our so-called Navaho speak?"

Vail said, "I'm sure you're just busting to tell me."

So Longarm said, "A *chindi* is a "haunt," an evil spirit, worse than an *anasazi*, or "ancient enemy," albeit Navaho and their Apache cousins would as soon avoid the deserted cliff dwellings built long before their time by the likely ancestors of the present-day Pueblos. According to some Diné or Nadéné speakers I've met friendly, knowing the right way-chants can get you past the regular haunts of just plain dead folk. But nobody ever gets past a *chindi* met up with in the uncertain light of dawn or dusk. So it's best not to stray from camp at such times and, if you *must* be out on the trail at dawn or dusk, it's best to shoot first at anything or anybody you think you see on the trail ahead, because it seems *chindi* are shape-shifters with the medicine to look like anybody, even a kinsman milling friendly at you all alone in tricky light along the trail."

Vail snorted more pungent smoke and observed, "That might explain some otherwise mysterious Indian skirmishes. But leave us not worry whether the dudes you'll be leading south of Fort Defiance are out to register and vaccinate real Quill Indians or shithouse rumors rising from some uncertainly mapped hole in the ground. The reasons I aim to send you southwest of Durango are twofold. To begin with, I want to sort of lose track of you whilst this scandal about the Hawker girl and her married lover simmers down. By the time you return, with any luck, they'll have sent the oversexed brat away to stricter supervision and whitewashed her sins to forgotten, or the story will have leaked, and it just won't matter how many lawmen might or might not know she was rescued from that love nest the other night!"

Longarm nodded and said, "That's one sensible reason. You said there might be two, boss?"

Vail said, "I did. I figured as long as you had to head

down that way you might as well check out another shit-house rumor that's crossed this desk more than once."

Leaning back in his swivel chair, Vail explained, "An uncharted canyon haunted by Indians dead or alive may be the least of our more serious problems. Leaving Durango on horseback as part of a medical expedition under an assumed name, you'll pass through the trail town of Animas Point. I want you to pass on through without telling even the town law who you're really riding for. Once you get your B.I.A. dudes wherever they want to go, and lead them safely back to Fort Defiance, I want you to part company with 'em, kill some time down that way 'til they're long gone, and drift back up to Animas Point alone and feeling blue as you confide you got fired just for helping yourself to some medical supplies and . . . Hell, you know how to look like a saddle tramp down on his luck along the owlhoot trail, don't you?"

Longarm said, "It'll serve Reporter Crawford right. But what am I supposed to be looking for in Animas Point as a shady character with a checkered past?"

Vail said, "Might not be there. On the other hand, more than one informant has reported the same thing without a chance to compare notes. So how do you feel about a haunted whorehouse, whether there's a haunted canyon down yonder or not?"

Longarm said he'd given up believing in any breed of haunt since the time he'd spooked himself as a kid in a graveyard with a little help from a barn owl. So he wanted to hear how one might go about haunting a whorehouse and asked whether the haunts were supposed to be he-spooks or she-spooks.

Vail sounded serious as he said, "That's what I want you to find out. As we both know, to our sorrow, those still poorly charted stretches of basin and range betwixt the Rockies and the Sierra Nevada are haunted for certain by outlaws ranging north and south from the Canadian to

35

Mexican lines. Save for a few civilized patches such as the Mormon Delta or the mining camps betwixt Virginia and Carson cities, out Nevada way, such nominal law as one might find in many an unincorporate township, such as Animas Point, can best be described as informal past common sense. Amimas Point ain't under the jurisdiction of any particular federal court, and we're stuck with the rumor emanating from the same because they keep coming our way through Durango."

Longarm gently but firmly insisted, "I never asked if we had the jurisdiction, Uncle Billy."

Vail said, "I was fixing to palm it off on Santa Fe before you got yourself in this mess over the Hawker brat. In sum, since you'll be down that way in any case, trail-town whores reported dead ten years or more ago are said to be entertaining owlhoot riders down yonder where neither the roads nor the laws of the land run certain. Did I mention how long some of the riders stopping by for a drink, a fuck or a few days flop in such friendly surroundings seem to have been reported dead and buried, long ago and far away?"

Longarm flicked more ash on the rug, shrugged, and said he'd look into the matter, even though he didn't buy a haunted whorehouse *or* a tribe of ghostly Indians.

So later that day the two of them were waiting at the Union Station for the broad guage Burlington from Chicago, figuring to show their charges from the B.I.A. to the hotel across the way to rest them some and wise them up about high desert in late summer before Longarm led them aboard the narrow guage for Durango after a good night's rest.

As the two lawman lounged on the platform, they were not aware they were being fish-eyed from inside the station by a pair of dedicated professional assassins. The younger and more edgy of the deadly pair was sure he could nail them both from the shadows of their vantage point and simply walk away through the gathering crowd.

But the older killer who'd recruited a face Longarm would never recognize warned, "You're not being paid to kill them both. Longarm is the only target, and he's not to die here in Denver, lest too many questions be inspired by such a dramatic event. You're to throw down on him well clear of me and my town. Weren't you paying attention when I said I wanted to show you who you were after and then, damnit, kill him *my* way?"

The younger killer shrugged and said, "The man who pays the piper calls the tune. I'll kill him your way if that's what you want. But it still sounds like a heap of bother."

Chapter 5

Neither Longarm nor Billy Vail were as surprised when the bunch from Washington showed up bone weary, grimy with locomotive soot and out of sorts from the consumption of stale sandwiches and warm beer or soda pop all the way across the plains from Chicago. The seven travel-weary newcomers consisted of the expedition leaders, Agent Martin Luther Thalmann and his tagalong wife, Miss Wilma; a spanking new surveying officer, Second Lieutenant H. R. Grover with his stake man, Sergeant Wynn, Corps of Engineers; and more important to any Indians they caught up with at the end of the wild rumor, a middle-aged Dr. Frank and two nurses, both Sisters, who he'd brought along to vaccinate all those Chindi Indians.

Wilma Thalmann seemed to feel she deserved to be admired in spite of all that soot on her face and fly ash in her likely brunette hair. The two nurses were younger built. Longarm suspected they might be passable once he got 'em cleaned up. So he pitched in to help with a whole heap of baggage as Billy Vail herded everyone across to those hotel suites he'd reserved for them in the name of Uncle Sam.

By the time the helpful Denver lawmen had them settled in a mite, Longarm had established the taller ash blond nurse answered to Sister Marsha Olan whilst the shorter chestnut-headed one was a Sister Fiona Manson, and neither seemed insulted when he suggested they might care to be shown the way to the lady's baths and steam room on the ground floor. They both agreed they could *eat* once they got all that road grime out of their poor hides. So that gave Longarm time to rejoin Billy Vail and the Thalmanns to ask how they felt about Chinee food that set well on uncertain stomachs, come supper time in just an hour or more.

Agent Thalmann didn't seem to notice, or care, that he and his woman resembled escapees from a minstrel show. He said he was anxious to get on down to that mysterious canyon country betwixt Fort Defiance and Canyon de Chelly. He pronounced "Chelly" to rhyme with "Shelly." Longarm hesitated. Then, seeing there was nobody else there but Billy Vail and Thalmann's own wife, Longarm quietly said, "No offense, sir, but over in the canyon country they pronounce 'Chelly' to rhyme with 'Shay,' or 'Chey.' "

To which the expedition leader imperiously replied, "Nonsense! I have always pronounced it to rhyme with 'Shelly' because it *does* rhyme with 'Shelly,' unless you're trying to tell me Kit Carson's famous victory over those Navaho raiders took place in some *other* Canyon de Chelly?"

Billy Vail had to look away as Longarm soberly replied, "Nossir. Colonel Carson fought and won the Battle of Canyon de Chelly back in '64. I wasn't there. So I can't say just how *he* might have pronounced it. But he did speak Spanish and married up with two Indian ladies in a row."

Agent Thalmann nodded smugly to insist, "He would certainly have pronounced 'Chelly' as he wrote it, in his own dispatches, to rhyme with 'Shelly,' just as I said."

Longarm murmured, "Ours not to reason why, and we still ain't settled on restaurant reservations for such a large party, sir."

Billy Vail cut in to say he'd handle it. Then he suggested Longarm might want to see to his own travel plans, seeing he wouldn't be out in the field in his more usual capacity. So Longarm said he'd be on his way, and as he was leaving he heard Wilma Thalmann asking Vail just what such a doubtless well-meant but argumentative young man did for them at the Denver federal building.

Longarm only heard the beginning as old Billy launched into a tale of a former Indian scout anxious to get back in the field after a spell of file-clerking. Longarm was too steamed to laugh out loud as he grumped off down Wynkoop Street, muttering darkly about lost tribes and haunted whorehouses indeed, dad blast that snippy Susan Hawkin and her teenaged twat!

Billy Vail had given Longarm a copy of Henry's typed up list of mysterious shadows from the past some said they'd spotted in or about a Madam Marlotte's house of ill fame on the outskirts of Animas Point overlooking the river flowing south from Durango betwixt ever rising walls of red Navaho sandstone. Informants gave the Madam's full name as *Virginia* Marlotte, which seemed to stretch coincidence a mite thin.

As he headed for a livery where he'd done business before, Longarm decided some poor trail-town whore had simply adopted the name out of admiration for a more famous and well-liked sporting gal of the Nevada silver fields. There was simply no way the one and original Virginia Marlotte could be running a whorehouse in Animal Point or anywheres else. For her gravestone over to Pioche, Nevada, was now a well-known tourist attraction, reading

"Here lies the body of Virginia Marlotte,
She was born a virgin and died a harlot.
For eighteen years she preserved her virginity.
That's a damned good record in this vicinity!"

The real Virginia Marlotte had died of pneumonia or, some said, the consumption. Longarm didn't see how she could be running any whorehouse, either way. [Whilst the rumors about poor old Madame Moustache were unfair as well as impossible. For before her recent suicide in Bodie the once attractive, but fuzzy-lipped, Madame Moustache had been a serious card dealer, not a whore, and rumors of the late Dora Hand selling her favors in Animas Point after she was shot in the bed of the mayor of Dodge by a would-be assassin seemed unkind. For the Dodge City papers had listed Dora Hand as a "singer" not a whore or even the mistress of Mayor Kelley.]

At the livery, Longarm hired a well-broken-in roping saddle, the rig you'd expect a drifter to ride along the owlhoot trail, lest some savvy spook at that haunted whorehouse have a description of a well-known Colorado rider who usually came in a tobacco tweed outfit astride an Army McClellen saddle. Longarm had been anxious to shed the federal dress-code duds he had to wear on officious duty. Clean but faded blue denim would do him fine in the Four Corners country in August, where the night winds might blow too cold for blue denim with the afternoon sunlight too blamed hot for any duds at all.

Like most experienced trailsmen, Longarm had long since learned heat was more likely than cold to lay one low in the southwest of a summer. When you got to feeling cold you could always build a fire or wrap something around you. But when you got to feeling too hot, there was nothing you could do but grit your teeth and bear it 'til things cooled off or you just up and died like a wriggle worm caught by the sun on a flagstone walk.

He toted the hired stock-saddle back to the hotel to store with the rest of the expedition gear in a baggage room. He meant to change into more practical duds and pick up his Winchester '73 and saddlebags when he went home for the night. He didn't recognise the cool ash blond in starched white linen at first. So he asked how come she seemed to be messing with a Saratoga trunk and offered to help her get it upstairs if it was her own.

Of course, as soon as she told him she was only out to check against busted glass, he recognized her from her voice as Sister Marsha Olan. It wouldn't have been polite to comment on how badly she'd really needed that bath and no doubt a sincere shampoo.

Longarm hadn't changed that much since they'd met across the way at the Union Station. So she addressed him as Mr. Crawford and he felt no call to argue as he shifted the heavy trunk into a handier position so she could open it with the help of a key ring and inspect inside, she explained, for travel breakage.

He saw why once he'd lifted the heavy lid out of the way for her. As he stared soberly down at all those corked test tubes of straw-colored serum nested in cotton waste, he observed she'd sure been planning to vaccinate a whole heap of Indians.

She nodded demurely but explained as she hunkered down to lift top trays out to probe deeper into her medical supplies that they naturally hoped other outlying tribesfolk would come in to be saved from the pox once Agent Thalmann had set up his Chindi Reservation. Then she asked what he was grinning about.

He wiped the silly grin off his face and politely explained he sort of doubted they'd find any Indians describing themselves as Chindi in the canyon lands betwixt Fort Defiance and Canyon de Chelly. "Most of the tribal designations used by your B.I.A. were given to the folk involved by their enemies. *Sioux* means a 'dirty sneak' in what you'd pronounce as Chippewa. They call themselves Ojibwa. I doubt any band speaking Diné or what you'd call Navaho would describe themselves as Chindi. They'll likely turn out to be Ho Hada or what the B.I.A. and Colorado State Guard describe as Ute. *Ute* is Navaho for 'highlander.' A *chindi* is a particularly nasty Navaho spook. So who do you reckon might have bestowed the name on some hold-out Quill Ho Hada hiding out on Navaho reserve?"

She thought, brightened, and said, "I see what you mean! They must be runaway Utes who didn't want to move out to the Utah Territory as we told them to and . . . Why do you pronounced Canyon de Chelly so oddly?"

Since she'd rhymed it with "Shelly," Longarm told her, not unkindly, she was the one who'd been saying it wrong. He quickly added, "Don't ask me why, Miss Marsha. I'm only going by the way folk who live in those parts pronounce it. Can't say just what Chelly means. It ain't proper Spanish. Must be Mex slang or some Indian word spelled Spanish with both the double *l* and *y* pronounced as we pronounce *y*. No white man had ever ridden in or out alive before Kit Carson and a mixed party of red and white riders, weary of Navaho raiding, tracked some home to their secret headquarters in Canyon de Chelly to whup 'em fair and square."

He wasn't paid to criticize other federal agencies, so he looked away to quietly mutter, "Ute scouts served Carson and the U.S. Army well against a common enemy, back when the Navaho were considered the bigger danger. So some Ho Hada might feel they have some right to sulk and lick their wounds up some uncharted canyon. Navaho sheepherders warned with arrow shots or worse to keep away might well report they'd encountered spooks in parts where no Navaho dwelt."

He thought he was muttering low when he added that

had it been up to him nobody would be pestering folk who only wanted to be left alone.

But she had sharp ears as well as a quick mind. So as she replaced a tray of serum, Marsha chided, "Have you ever watched a child of any race die of smallpox, ah, Custis? The Mandans along the upper Missouri only wanted to be left alone, but wandering traders will wander in, and after the pox swept through back in the '30s, there weren't any Mandan left to leave alone."

She shut the lid as she soberly added, "The pity of it all was that we'd had safe vaccination against smallpox for more than thirty years as it was wiping out the Mandan, and not doing a thing to make Pawnee or their Sioux enemies happy! You see, the Turks had discovered a not-too-safe attempt at immunization way back when, with the odds on it *giving* you a fatal dose of smallpox instead of preventing it around sixty-forty in your favor. So folk like George Washington just took their chances and in his case managed to live through a natural infection. But then, in 1796, Edward Jenner discovered he could safely vaccinate people against the plague by . . ."

"What's going on in here?" demanded an imperious voice Queen Victoria herself might have been impressed by.

So the two of them rose from beside the Saratoga to face the music in the form of the cleaned up Wilma Thalmann, who looked way better after her own bath and shampoo, but not as grand as she seemed to think she looked, because nobody could have.

The beautiful bitch announced, "We'll have none of *that* as long as I'm in charge of this expedition, Sister Marsha!"

Marsha Olan just blushed and stammered. So it was Longarm's job to politely tick his hat brim and reply, "Your pleasure, ma'am, and may I ask what civil service rank you might hold before we get into explaining ourselves sneaking into this baggage room with our own blamed baggage?"

The imperious brunette flinched as if she'd been slapped across her pretty face with a fly swatter before she sputtered, "How *dare* you speak to your superiors like that! I'll have you know I am the *wife* of Martin Luther Thalmann of the Bureau of Indian Affairs!"

Longarm nodded pleasantly and said, "Met an army colonel's daughter who thought that meant she outranked me, one time. The delusion is occasioned by the tendency of enlisted men to butter up the boss. I fear that ain't my style, no offense. But even though I don't take my orders from you, or even your husband, unless they make more sense, I will tell you, since you *asked*, I just brung yonder roping saddle in to store with the rest of the expedition gear. Sister Marsha, here, was inspecting her smallpox kit to make sure the baggage smashers hadn't busted any test tubes. When I expressed some interest she was kind enough to show and tell. Are there any other questions?"

Wilma Thalmann was blushing, now, as she stammered, "I just came to tell Sister Marsha we're all going to supper now at a restaurant that kind Marshal Vail suggested."

When she added, "The others are waiting on us, dear," the younger ash blond lit out like a scalded cat, leaving the beautiful bitch and Longarm alone for the moment. So she tried in a more soothing tone to say, "I'm sorry if I may have seemed short with the two of you, just now. It's simply that I feel responsible for our two young Sisters and, well, since no harm's been done, we'll not have to mention it to my husband, now that we all understand one another."

Longarm smiled wolfishly and replied, "Lady, you don't understand this child for horse apples. What would your husband do if you told him you'd caught me in here throwing a Roman orgy with both your Sisters and that

46

sort of sissy looking Lieutenant Grover? What *could* he do? Fire me? Be my guest, Your Majesty! I never wanted to ride the Four Corners country in flash-flood season to begin with, and now that I've seen what a chickenpeck outfit this is, I'd have already *quit* if I wasn't curious about the way this story ends."

Chapter 6

Some ancient Roman had decreed that the wagon ruts on all those roads that led to Rome should follow the same four-foot-eight guage, which had likely made more sense in Roman numerals. So the wheels of wagons, carriages and railroad cars still followed that same standard guage, save in Russia where they didn't even use the same calendar, or over in the high country where a yard-wide narrow guage was easier to wrap around a mountain. So the dinky cars of D & RGRR Western Division only had seats along one side of the narrow off-center aisles, and Longarm found himself seated next to Second Lieutenant Grover, who seemed unusually pissed off at the world that morning, even for a second lieutenant.

From the way others had greeted him when he showed up that morning in faded denim jeans and jacket with his .44-40 worn openly and a Winchester '73 cradled over his left forearm, Longarm had gotten the impression they had him down as one of those crusty frontier guides a good Christian simply had to put up with, wearily smiling, if one expected to be shown to good fishing or kept out of the poison ivy. After trying in vain to start a conversation about army life, Longarm excused himself to amble back to the open platform for a solitary smoke and more serious thought.

He'd gone over that typed up list at home the night before. No matter how you sliced it. It made no sense. Longarm could come up with dozens of ways a trail-town whorehouse out in the middle of nowheres could *appear* to be staffed with famous dead whores. Ingenious or desperate whore mongers were forever coming up with novel attempts to attract more trade. Sheer silk stockings and the high heels now the fashion of high society had been invented to show the legs of whores to more tempting advantage. Whores, like actresses, were forever changing their names to those of more famous women or characters from books or even fairy tales. That one poor drab up Leadville way had made a fortune as Miss Cinderella by the time her customers had noticed she really *was* awfully plain. So the procuress calling herself Madam Virginia Marlotte could have named her live-in help Dora Hand, Madame Moustache and such just to attract attention, with unwholesome overtones of graveyard mold to pique the interest of jaded customers.

But whilst you saw a lot of decadent spooky shit around whorehouses you weren't supposed to see dead men patronizing whores, whether dead or alive. So what could have possessed not one but two informants to report they'd seen Black Jack Slade sipping cider with Dora Hand in the taproom of Madam Marlotte's in Animas Point?

As he got his cheroot going, alone on the platform, Longarm assured, "Whores acting loco ain't unusual when business is slow. Men coming in off the street disguised as famous dead outlaws would be illogical as well as unusual! Why in thunder would any rider, whether innocent or guilty, set out to get himself shot on sight as advised by old dead or alive posters? Riders of the owlhoot trail try to pass in town for more honest gents, not wanted by the law. What sort of an asshole would try to pass himself off as a *wanted* outlaw, no matter who he'd started out as, wanted for whatever! Black Jack Slade was a murderer strung up for his crimes. That other report about the late William P. Longley having his beard trimmed in Animas Point before paying a call on Madam Marlotte would only work if some even more murderous mad dog had something even worse to hide!"

It surely was a poser, Longarm repeated to himself as they entered the first of many a tunnel their dinky shay engine was fixing to haul them through on the way to Durango. Longarm removed the cheroot from his lips and shut his eyes against fly ash as their train rattled underground through concentrated coal smoke. When they came out into the sunlight on the far side, Longarm found he was no longer alone on the platform.

The baby-faced survey officer, Grover, had followed him back to the platform, he said, because they had a bone to pick.

Drawing himself fully erect, and still standing nigh a head shorter than Longarm, Grover said, "The terms are perforce up to you, Mr. Crawford. But it's only right to warn you I was on the boxing team at the Point, and I've twice scored a possible on the pistol range."

Longarm smiled down uncertainly to reply, "Back up and run that by me again, Lieutenant. What could I have said, inside, just now, to inspire an affair of honor, for Chrissake?"

The kid snapped, "Nothing, to my face! But I understand you have implied behind my back that I'm a queer!"

The easy way out was tempting. But there'd been two witnesses and it hurt worse to be caught in a lie. So Longarm gravely replied to the charge with, "Nobody can deny you're a second lieutenant, but I was out of line when I took it out on another man because I was pissed off at a woman. So I'm sincerely sorry, and I apologize for intimating you might be less a man than myself, Lieutenant."

The kid said he'd still fight Longarm if he thought he was a sissy.

Longarm sighed and said, "Had I wanted to fight you, I'd have never said I was in the wrong. For the record I never called you a queer. But what I did say was foolish and mean-spirited. But show me one man who's never shot his mouth off mean and stupid, and I'll show you a fucking liar!"

Lieutenant Grover laughed despite himself and admitted he knew he looked sort of young and girlish for an army engineer. Then he held out a hand, and Longarm meant it when he said, "You look manly enough for me, Lieutenant, and if I ever *do* stage a Roman orgy with the nursing staff of this expedition, you're invited to pitch in and help me out with the chore!"

"Is *that* how you pictured me to Miss Wilma?" laughed the army man in restored good humor, adding, "Which one do I get, the blond or the chestnut?"

Longarm smiled less certainly and opined, "Before I put my fool foot in my mouth again, I'd best explain neither Sister has given me any cause to invite them to as much as a tea party, and Miss Wilma will be watching over the two of them like a biddy hen with a mean streak. I told her to mind her own beeswax and leave me be. But I could afford to. I don't ride for the B.I.A., and I don't give a shit if Agent Thalmann chooses to go on with another guide."

The younger officer grimaced and said, "My stake man and me are on loan from the War Department, and to tell the truth we're both about fed up with the arrogant son of a bitch and his bitch-on-wheels wife. What do you suppose could be wrong with that mismatched pair, Mr. Crawford?"

Longarm said he'd feel more comfortable if the shave-tail would call him "Buck," which was only bullshit when you studied on it, and went on to opine, "Him being well over forty and her pushing thirty could be part of it. I noticed when I was alone with just the two of 'em, he can't unbend enough to admit he don't know everything in front of her. She's likely suffering from the all-too-familiar delusions of the Colonel's Lady, a malady familiar to officers with mebbe a tad more experience with garrison politics."

The shavetail said he'd already met the Colonel's Lady, more than once at more than one army post and explained, "Miss Wilma doesn't puzzle me as much as her older and more experienced Indian agent. I made the mistake aboard the train from Washington to Chicago via New York of telling him he was reading an army survey map upside down. I feared he was about to suffer a brain stroke or hit me with a ruler. Then he recovered and said he'd of course known he was reading the map from north to south because we'd be riding north to south out of the Ute Reserve in southwest Colorado. But why would he have gone all purple in the face like so if he hadn't been made to look like a fool?"

Longarm said, "Can't say for certain about Agent Thalmann. I was out this way when an Agent Meeker, Nathan C., arrived at the White River Agency, north of Durango, to elevate and enlighten the North Ute, as he put it in his earnest, humorless way."

The army man said, "I read about the Meeker Massacre and the Battle of White River in the *Army Times*. You say all that confusion was the fault of a cross-grained Indian agent who wouldn't take advice?"

Longarm paused to relight the cheroot he'd allowed to go out before he soberly observed, "Fair is fair, and Agent Meeker might have had a heap of trouble with a cross-grained sixty-year-old chief they called Colorow and a meaner and younger war chief called Nicaagat by his people, who called themselves Ho, not Utes. But Agent

53

Meeker knew better and described Nicaagat as a trouble-maker he called Jack and never asked why Nicaagat came in for his agency handouts in his army scout uniform, sporting army medals he'd won scouting for General Crook during Red Cloud's War. It pissed Agent Meeker to have the younger Ho, or Utes, admire Nicaagat and his kinsman, Colorow, in spite of Meeker having chosen to make an amiable old cuss Meeker called Douglas the nominal chief of the White River band."

The young shavetail showed he read more than the *Army Times* when he asked, "Can an Indian agent do that? I thought most Indians sort of elected their own chiefs."

Longarm nodded and conceded, "Election is a close enough term if you toss out majority rule. None of the warrior societies hold what we'd call an election and agree to all abide by the results. When a Quill Indian hasn't agreed you're his chief you *ain't* his chief as far as he's concerned. Makes it a bitch to work out treaties, fair or otherwise, with nations of such free thinkers."

He got his cheroot going again as the train rattled on and told the greenhorn, "Agent Meeker shared the common delusion that Indians had to do what a chief they'd never voted for told them to do. Douglas, who's Indian name was Quinkent by the way, had never been a chief to begin with. He was an easy-going horse trader, rich by Indian standards and hence popular with the ladies, but having no standing with the younger men of a proud fighting nation."

Grover whistled silently and said, "Then all that trouble we had a few summers back was caused by an opinionated agent backing the wrong faction in a tribal dispute?"

Longarm grimaced and replied. "If only. Meeker managed to get the whole bunch sore at him. He began by demanding they call him Father Meeker, since they were his savage children, and held back on rations when some of his wards decided to call him Nate, or Nick, or worse.

Indian humor tends to be sardonic and direct. But he still might have made a go of it had he stopped to consider how a red or white man was supposed to make a go of it at subalpine altitudes in what most Indians still call the Shining Mountains."

They went through another tunnel, and the shavetail naturally got a cinder in his eye. So as he fished it out for Grover with the corner of a clean kerchief Longarm laconically continued, "Unless you have a high-grade mine in the Colorado high country, you fish, hunt, trap and raise stock. Grazing 'em on the brief rich grass of summer and foddering 'em in barns or box canyons during the long cold mountain winters. Wild berries thrive better than specimen fruit trees. The only grains that can ripen betwixt late and early mountain frosts being barley and oats. But Agent Meeker had his appointed chief tell his savage children to plow under their few level patches of pasture to plant corn and taters. He ordered them to sell off or shoot their pony herds and replace them with dairy cows.

"By this time, even his tame horse-trading Douglas was trying to point out the so-called Ute had no use for dairy products of any kind, prefering white flour instead of cream in their trading post coffee. But Agent Meeker was determined Colorow, the chief the Indians *listened* to, was a mean drunk, and when Meeker cut off further rations and allotments until his savage children shaped up or shipped out, it was Nicaagat who led the uprising after Meeker wired the Utes had risen, and he needed the troops to crush the out-of-control savages and arrest the ringleaders.

"He must not have known retired army scouts could read telegrams. The accounts of later events, you read in the *Army Times* got all but a few details right. No mention was made of the gang rapes of Meeker's wife, daughter and a teenager visiting 'em, recovered weeping but not damaged beyond repair after Nate Meeker, seven agency

55

hands, plus a heap of army and Indian riders had bit the dust. Colorow was sent to Leavenworth whilst everything and everyody else got whitewashed.

"It turned out Meeker had lied like a rug about Indians setting forest fires, burning out white settlers and such. But of course the White River Utes and some bands who'd had nothing to do with the sad events at the White River Agency were frog-marched west across the Green in Utah Territory, where it serves the Mormons right for saying Indians are human beings who could be lost tribes of Israel, to the mind of our current Governor Pitkin."

The shavetail handed the kerchief back with a nod of thanks as he asked, "Then you're suggesting some of these Colorado Utes could be a tad displeased with the Great White Father, these days?"

Longarm grimaced and replied, "Totally pissed off would be the term *I'd* use. I wasn't there, but I have Ho Hada pals who rode with Carson against the Navaho, with Crook against the Lakota when Red Cloud was winning, and agreed to the treaty of 1863 signed by Doc Evans, the then-governor of Colorado Territory and Ouray or Arrow, a literate high chief as fluent as me in English and Spanish. The deal he made conceded all the high country east of the Great Divide, including all the then-known gold fields, to his Saltu Taibo brothers, a sort of contradiction in terms but that's how treaties read."

He snorted smoke out both nostrils to add, "The treaty agreed no whites would pass over, settle or reside amongst the Ho Hada or Utes west of the divide. But that was asking the impossible, and you say you read about all the gunplay in the *Army Times*, so what does it matter how anyone feels about such ancient history?"

The army engineer said, "It's my understanding we'll be joined at the end of the rails in Durango by Indian horse wranglers and camp workers from the nearby La

Plata Agency. Correct me if I'm wrong, but isn't that a *Ute* agency?"

Longarm sighed and said, "It is. Southern Ute. Not quite as pissed off at us as Northern Ute, but not at all happy about the way they were rewarded for licking the Navaho for us that time!"

Chapter 7

Pullman made no narrow-guage dining cars. So they stopped for noon dinner at Canon City, pronounced Canyon but spelled Spanish without a tilde over the first N. The D & RGRR didn't give passengers time for table conversation and neither Sister might have managed her coffee had not Longarm shown them how to saucer and blow such scalding joe. Strong enough, cold, to tan leather.

When the chestnut-haired Fiona Manson asked where he'd learned such a clever trick, Longarm confided, "Used to herd cows. You don't get this much time off for dinner, herding cows."

That was about all he got to say to either before the engine bell was summoning them back aboard for the still considerable rail trip ahead.

Denver and Durango were an awkward distance apart for a line that ran no sleeping cars. Back aboard the train, Longarm found himself facing the two Sisters and seated next to their boss, Doc Frank, once they'd shifted that seat-back forward to ride backwards, side by side.

Doc Frank was a friendly-faced cuss of around forty with curly black hair to match his close-cropped beard.

Longarm didn't ask which of the Sisters might be with him. As they rode along, it seemed Doc Frank had agreed to treat them like kid sisters. For if he hadn't, would it have seemed sort of dumb to Longarm when the sawbones showed him tintypes of his wife and baby daughter back in Baltimore. The tintype described the doc's woman as about the same age but not as snotty as old Wilma Thalmann, seated at the far end with her know-it-all Indian agent.

In between, mixed with some other passengers, Lieutenant Grover and Sergeant Wynn were marveling at the mountain scenerey out the windows, consulting an army compass and a survey chart as they tried to decide where in the hell they might be. Judging distances or even north from south could get tough in the Shining Mountains, where neither rails nor trails ran straight enough to matter for the better part of a mile.

Doc Frank confided he'd been boning up on "the Indian language" in preperation of his medical mission to the Chindi. When Longarm asked who'd told him which dialect the mysterious Chindi spoke, the sawbones looked confounded and replied, "Regular *Indian*, I suppose. I understand some bands may have different *accents* but won't a *squaw* and her *papoose* benefit as much from vaccination whether we pronounce that one way or another? What's so funny?"

Longarm wiped the smile off his face and said, "It's all right to call a Cheyenne *esquaw* a *squaw*. But Lakota have been known to get surly, hearing their *weyahs* referred to by an Algonquin term mountain men and soldiers-blue applied to Indian . . . business women. What you've been studying as regular Indian, no offense, was the Eastern Algonquin our kind recorded first and never bothered to study further on the way west. Arapaho, Blackfoot, Cheyenne and Plains Cree savvy Algonquin, sort of. But unless they've been reading James Fenimore Cooper, few western nations would have the least notion of your meanings if you spoke to them of *wigwams, moccasins, tomahawks* and such. With any luck the unregistered Indians you're out to vaccinate will be Ho or Uto-Aztec speakers. It's tough but possible for a white man to learn *that* lingo. All bets are off if them Chindi turn out to be Diné or Navaho speakers. You show me a white man claiming fluency in Diné, and I'll show you a big fibber."

"You mean there's that much difference in Indian accents?" asked the perky chestnut-haired Sister Fiona.

Longarm patiently repeated, "They don't speak different accents. They speak different languages entire. This anthrowhatsits lady I . . . ah, guided through some cliff dwellings a spell back told me she felt sure *most* American Indian lingoes seem closely related as those old country lingoes descended from Ancient Aryan, such as English, Dutch, French and even Hindu. That don't mean a Lakota can understand a Cheyenne any more than a Frenchman can understand an Englishman. But at least they share some grammar and a few words. Ask a Lakota what he's riding he'll describe it as a *tashunka* or mayhaps a *shunka wakan*. Ask an Arapaho, and he'll assure you he's aboard his good old *ponokah meta*. The point is that both Indian lingos agree a horse is a horse or mayhaps a spirit dog. But according to that linguist gal I just mentioned, Eskimo and Nadéné dialects rival one another as to complexicated grammar. Ask a Navaho or Apache how to say *horse* and he'll ask if you mean a horse you can both see, a horse out of sight, a horse that belongs to an enemy, a horse that belongs to a friend, and so on 'til a white man's ears get too confounded to care."

Sister Fiona said she hoped the Chindi spoke Ho and asked Longarm to teach them some.

He smiled wryly and replied, "Ain't got the time if I was fluent. But I understand we'll be picking up Ho-speaking help at the South Ute agency and you'll hardly need to tell a Ho speaker you happen to be vaccinating much more than that it's *puha*, meaning good medicine in Ho."

Doc Frank frowned to say he'd understood the "Indian" word for medicine was *panisee*.

Longarm said, "It is, in Algonquin. In Sioux-Hokan you'd want to say *wakan*. It's still *puha* in Uto-Aztec."

The older man sighed, "You're right, we're talking about entirely differant languages. You must think I'm a real *schlemiel*!"

Longarm soberly replied, "Not if that means foolish, Doc. Nobody starts out knowing everything. The first time I was told to saddle a cavalry mount, I had to ask how. The first time I was warned not to camp in a desert wash, I had to ask why. The real fools are the ones who don't want to be told how or why."

"Why don't we want to camp in a desert wash?" asked Sister Fiona, and Longarm just nodded when Doc Frank told her, "Flash floods. I was just reading up on desert travel and they say more people die by drowning than from heat stroke in the canyon lands ahead."

Longarm didn't insult a grown man by praising his common sense as if he'd been a bright schoolboy.

But the older man was suddenly aware of Longarm's forbearance and flushed like a schoolboy, turning to stare out at the passing mountain scenery. The ash-blond Sister Marsha had noticed, too, going by her Mona Lisa expression. Sister Fiona just said, "Oh."

Longarm decided it was time for another smoke on that open platform. As he passed the Thalmanns, he got a funny look from the bitchy brunette Wilma. He was even more puzzled when she followed him out, alone, to observe she'd never expected to spend the rest of her life aboard a narrow guage in the Rocky Mountains.

Longarm assured her they'd be stopping for supper and the night at Del Rio, explaining, "They don't like to run in the dark around such uncertain curves in landslide country, Miss Wilma. After a good night's rest in Del Rio, we'll rise and shine for a short morning's run into Durango and have the whole afternoon to set up for further travel on horseback. Do you mind if I smoke, ma'am?"

She said, "Go right ahead. I don't mind *minor* vices. It's real trouble I worry about, and you do seem to make a habit of worrying me that way!"

Longarm left his tobacco be as he asked what in thunder she might be accusing him of, now.

She sniffed, "That's for you to say. I've no idea why that shabby cowboy has been glaring at you like a cat about to pounce. But as I told you back in Denver, I'll have no messy nonsense on my way to our new Chindi Reservation!"

Longarm honestly replied, "Miss Wendy, I've not idea what you're talking about! I ain't seen any cowboys or even Indians glaring at me of late!"

She sniffed and said, "Of course you haven't. He hasn't been looking at you like that to your face. He's been trying to hide his true feelings, unaware of my own experienced eye for trouble at any distance. He's dressed in a darker version of your range worker's costume, with a taller crown to his black sombrero and his six-shooter worn low on his right hip. In one of those busky dusky holsters . . . ?"

Longarm smiled thinly to reply, "*Buscadero* holster is the term you were groping for, ma'am. The rig is named for a Mexican term for a cuss who's hunting for trouble. They still sell 'em to kid cowboys out to look more dangerous than they might feel. How old would you say my secret admirer might be?"

She shrugged and said, "Anywhere between a tough looking teenager and a baby-faced thirty year old. Dame nature is so unfair that way about you boys. You get to look young far longer than you deserve!"

Longarm asked where inside the mystery man might be sitting. She told him she'd last spied the youthful dark figure with the big black sombrero and *buscadero* gun rig staring at his back through the door glass at the other end of their car. He nodded and said he'd best go ask the young cuss what he wanted.

As he moved to step around her, Wilma Thalmann blocked his way, gasping, "No! I told you I didn't want any trouble on my expedition!"

Then the train tore into another tunnel and she was all over him in the smoky darkness, clutching at his demin and kissing him French.

Longarm kissed her back as any man would have but then they were back out in the light of reason and he shoved clear of her, snorting, "*I* don't want no trouble on this expedition, neither, so keep your cotton picking claws off my cotton jeans before your husband gets to ask what's going on out here!"

She demurely explained she and her husband had certain understandings about a healthy young woman's needs but added, "That's not why I kissed you, ah, Buck. We may or may not talk about that later. Right now I only have to convince you you don't want to start anything with that sinister stranger up in the next car!"

He asked, "How come? Seeing I don't know who he might be or what he might want?"

She insisted, "He hates you! I could tell!"

Longarm shrugged and said, "Mebbe. No offense but I've noticed how you like to tell. Whether he's after me or innocent as the driven snow, it makes more sense to have it out with him aboard a train filled with witnesses than on the dark streets of Del Rio or, even worse, them rimrocked canyon lands beyond!"

She still said, "Don't go!" and he still went, not looking at her husband or the others as he strode the swaying off-center aisle with a dry mouth and a tightness in the chest that was likely caused by the high altitude.

He knew that if Wilma had been telling the truth, the mysterious stranger with the low-slung six-gun could be waiting between cars on a platform ahead. There was no sane way to go blasting through sliding doors without the least notion who might be on the other side, or how come. So Longarm took a deep breath, grasped the brass latch with his left hand, and slid the door open to scoot through and crab to one side as he drew his .44-40.

He found himself alone and feeling foolish on an empty platform, facing another and the sliding door beyond. So he stood there a spell with his back to the bulkhead, letting his heart slow down from full gallop to a more comfortable lope.

He was fixing to move on when the door behind him slid wider and he almost threw down on Sister Marsha when she stepped through it to join him out there, gasping, "Buck! What's happening? Why are you aiming that gun like that?"

He urgently replied, "I ain't aiming at nobody, yet. Go back inside. I'll be proud to tell you all about it, farther along!"

She slid the door behind her shut, insisting, "I saw Miss Wilma follow you out that other door to that other platform! What did she want with you? Is she still trying to start some trouble for us?"

Longarm said, "If that's it, she's a crazy bitch beyond the call of duty! I know she tried to cause trouble betwixt Lieutenant Grover and me. She could be out to cause trouble betwixt me and a totally innocent stranger. I want you to go back inside so's I don't have to worry about nobody but me as I find out!"

She pleaded, "Let me fetch those two army men to back you up! You don't have to face down anyone aboard this train alone!"

Longarm shook his head and soberly said, "You're wrong, Sister Marsha. Neither the lieutenant nor his stakeman have a chip on this table, either way. If Miss Wilma's only trying to stir up trouble, I don't need no backup. If her warning's sincere, it's still best to settle up man-to-man. He's not about to admit he's after me, facing three-to-one odds. He'll just assure me a trouble-making woman got things wrong, and I'll have no choice but to buy that, true or false, until he's ready to make his move at some future time and place more favorable to him. So do like I say. I mean it, Sister Marsha!"

She turned with a strangled sob to duck back inside as Longarm stepped across to the other platform and eased to the sliding door of the next car. He knew that anyone expecting his face in the door glass could be set up to fire through the thin wood paneling. So he stood to one side, grasped the brass latch, and slid the door open as boldly as if he were on officious railroad business.

When nothing happened, he stepped sideways to enter the car beyond with his six-gun held politely down his right leg.

He got odd looks, of course, from more than one passenger. At the far end, a total stranger wearing a big, black, ten-gallon Stetson was reading the *Rocky Mountain News*, or pretending to.

As Longarm moved along the off-center aisle, he reholstered his .44-40. As he did so, a mining man riding with a fat lady in a mother hubbard asked if they might be in for some trouble.

Longarm said he didn't know yet as he moved on, eyes fixed on the stranger in the big black hat and gun hand ready to slap leather some more as he could only hope the stranger hadn't already drawn behind the seat-back betwixt the two of them.

Chapter 8

Odds such as that were the price one had to pay for a clear conscience. As the seated newspaper reader seemed to become aware of Longarm and looked up with a puzzled smile. Longarm said, "Howdy."

The man in black denim replied, "Howdy yourself. Am I supposed to know you?"

Longarm sat sideways, uninvited, in the empty seat ahead so's he could address the stranger across the back with a left elbow atop the same and his right hand casually resting on his gun grips as he said in reply, "I was fixing to ask you the same question. I've been given to understand you've been staring at my back a lot, of late."

The younger or more baby-faced stranger in black cocked a brow to remark, "That's odd. You don't look Mexican. But the last time I was invited to this waltz, I was 'tending a barrio dance in El Paso."

He adopted a vaudeville Mex accent to intone, "I mean you no disrespect, Señor. But for why ju been looking at the *mujer* of my cousin, Ramon, eh?"

Longarm soberly replied, "I'm still working on that. I'd be best described as Buck Crawford. I'm headed into the canyon lands with the B.I.A. party the next car up. Now it's your turn."

The stranger casually opened his black denim bolero jacket wider to expose an encircled star of German silver pinned to the front of his blue work shirt as he easily replied, "They call me Pecos Moran. Corporal Pecos Moran of the Texas Rangers. I'd heard you all were on your way south from Durango. Been wondering whether I ought to ask if I could ride with you-all as far as a trail town called Animas Point."

Longarm took his first deep breath for quite a spell before he said, "I ain't in command, but I don't see why not. I'll ask Agent Thalmann. Albeit I suspect the final answer might be up to his wife, and before you throw in with us, be advised the lady is a dedicated crazy cunt!"

Pecos Moran asked if they were talking about the older but not bad looking brunette in the ecru riding habit. When Longarm nodded, the Texan dryly observed, "Thought she might be the type to go through a man's pockets once she'd fucked him to sleep. But, Lord, don't them mean-hearted ones fuck the best? So what about the other two, the pert little roan and the cooler-looking palomino?"

Longarm smiled thinly and said, "She *was* telling the truth when she allowed you'd been staring. The younger gals are Sisters, out to vaccinate some Indians, Lord willing, the creeks don't rise and we ever *find* 'em. What's inspired your trip to Animas Point, a tad outside the juristiction of Texas, if you don't mind my asking?"

The man wearing a Texas Ranger badge said, "I don't mind anybody asking. Mean to pay a courtesy call on the town law the minute I ride in with not one but three wanted fliers. I'd be proud to show you, if you like."

Longarm allowed he had nothing better to read. So the Texan reached inside his bolero to produce three wanted posters of varied stock and dimensions. As he handed them across the seat-back, he casually asked if Longarm might be the Law as well.

"Just a paper-pusher assigned as a guide because I scouted for the cav in my misspent youth," Longarm lied as he perused the wanted posters and managed not to let his feelings show.

It wasn't easy. He knew for a fact all three posters were stale, and the three killers in question had been hanged, official, within recent memory.

Since he'd asked some trick questions in the line of duty in his own times at bat, Longarm soberly said, as he handed the papers back, "I could be wrong, of course. But it seems to me I read in the *Police Gazette* how your own state of Texas just hanged that one called Pronto Cruz for crimes too numerous to mention."

Putting the papers away, Moran easily replied, "All three of 'em are supposed to be dead. But Cruz is a fucking greaser, and all tall, skinny Anglos dressed cow tend to pass for one another at a distance and, in the meantime, all three of these old boys have been seen alive and well in Animas Point by paid snitches Texas has always felt she could rely on."

Hardly daring to believe his own luck, Longarm asked in a desperately casual tone what might make Animas Point such a gathering place for outlaws wanted far and wide.

Moran shrugged and said, "That's one of the things I mean to ask about, once I get there. I might well be on a wild-goose chase. Other lawman before me have already been there. Town law dismisses rumors of wild parties at the one big whorehouse in town as incomprehensible bullshit. But where there's smoke, there's fire, and why should one more or less trustworthy saddle-bum after another report more action than the town fathers seem willing to own up to?"

Longarm agreed he'd been through small clannish

towns with secrets to hide against strangers as he silently congratulated Billy Vail on what he'd first regarded as a needlessly complexicated plan. For the Texan had just confirmed Billy's suspicion that a lawman riding in from outside with his badge pinned on seemed likely to get a runaround.

Knowing poor Sister Marsha was sweating bullets in the next car ahead, Longarm suggested, "I'll tell you what. We'll be stopping in Del Rio for supper and a flop before sundown. Why don't you ease in on us in the hotel restaurant, and meanwhile I'll have put in a word for you with Agent Thalmann. I'm sure that in spite of the bitch he's stuck with, he'll want your extra gun hand along as we ride into such uncertain surroundings."

They shook on it across the seat-back and Longarm rose to rejoin the worried Marsha and the others. Before he got to the far door, he could see both those army men regarding him warily through the glass.

As he joined them on the platform, Marsha circled around Sergeant Wynn to grab hold of Longarm, sobbing, "Oh, thank God! I was so worried!"

Smiling wryly at Lieutenant Grover, Longarm said, "I asked her not to pester you. But, thanks, and you can put them guns away, now. He turned out to be a Texas Ranger, headed the same way on his own beeswax, and wasn't that thoughtful of Miss Wilma?"

The three of them agreed with relieved smiles that one had to admire such dedication to troublemaking and, as it to prove their point, the four of them were subjected to a puzzled look down the length of the car when Wilma Thalmann spotted what she no doubt considered a plot against her, with some justification.

The party broke up grinning when Longarm and the ash-blond sat down with Sister Fiona and Doc Frank as the army men moved on to resume their own empty seats ahead.

The perky but not as bright Sister Fiona asked what all that hustle and bustle had been about. Longarm would have fibbed. Marsha leaned toward her fellow nurse and the doc to confide, "That nasty Miss Wilma just tried to get Buck into a fight with a Texas Ranger. I told you how she as much as accused the two of us back in Denver, but maybe now you'll listen! What are we ever going to do about such a dreadful woman?"

The older and wiser Doc Frank sighed and said, "Confidential, not a thing. There's no legal way for an underling to get back at such a woman when she's sleeping with the boss. One pillow conversation after a . . . pillow fight can undo all the damage we could do her if we presented a united front, with everyone's clothes on!"

Longarm said that seemed about the size of it and soothed, "If it's any comfort, the lady has exposed her position by firing from cover too soon and too directsome. Poor Mr. Othello never might have been slickered into killing his innocent wife by that two-face Mr. Iago had his secret enemy been so up-front nasty."

He leaned back and let Doc Frank explain that all they had to do, along with those two army men, was to ignore the silly bitch, as if she was the little boy who cried wolf.

Sister Fiona asked, "What if she cries wolf and there's really a wolf, or say a hostile man or beast in the rough country we'll be heading into if ever this blamed train takes us to the end of this blamed line?"

"Let's hope they scalp her first," Longarm suggested. It was Marsha who pointed out the little boy who'd cried wolf was the one the wolf et first.

So they conversed about other worries, and it only seemed a million years before they finally hissed to a stop at Del Rio to change trains after a warm meal and good night's sleep, come morning.

Del Rio means "of the river," and so there were two Del Rios worth mention beside the brawling brown Rio

71

Grande. But Del Rio, Colorado, overlooked the furiously frothing coffee-with-cream river near the head-waters of a mightly long Rio Grande, which means "big river," with Del Rio, Texas, way the hell downstream.

The evening air was still balmly, despite the altitude, when Longarm slipped away from the other passengers supping at the Denver and Rio Grande Western Hotel to sneak a progress report to his home office from the nearby Western Union.

Since he was working undercover, his banal night letter, allowing for more words than usual at reduced rates, was in code and addressed to Billy Vail's wife at his home on Capitol Hill, under her maiden name. Mrs. Vail would know who her nephew, Buck, had to be. Longarm had to smile as he pictured her handing it to her man whilst clucking like a biddy hen about the hired help one had to put up with since the Emancipation Proclamation.

As he was paying for the message from his own pocket, even at night letter rates, lest anyone question a collect wire sent at government expense, Longarm glanced up to see a familiar face reflected in the glass of the telegrapher's corner cage in the dinky office. When Pecos Moran's eyes met Longarm's, secondhand, the Texan entered to belly up to the cage alongside him, observing, "Great minds seem to run in the same channels. I take it you just wired Austin to see if I'm real?"

"Never occured to me," Longarm lied, adding, "Since you ask . . ." before he called in to the clerk, "Would you mind telling this poor suspicious cuss where I just paid you to send that night letter?"

The clerk said, "I don't mind if you don't mind. You just now sent a night letter to an aunt in Denver, wishing her a happy birthday, Mr. Crawford."

So Longarm thanked him and told the Texan, "There you go. Why would I suspect you of doodly shit, Pecos? Have you got something dirty in mind for me?"

Moran dryly replied, "Didn't you know? I was fixing to backshoot you as I followed you here from the hotel, but I lost my nerve and now I got to send my own night letter to Austin if you don't mind."

Longarm said, "Western Union's all yours, now that I'm done with it. When you get back to the hotel, I'll introduce you to Thalmann and the others. I mentioned you aboard the train this afternoon, and not even that bitch-on-wheels could come up with an excuse to refuse an extra gun hand riding with us through Indian country."

So that was how things went through the early part of the evening. The three ladies retired first after some gabbing in the lobby. Then Agent Thalmann excused himself, no doubt to help his shapely bitch turn down the covers. Pecos Moran allowed he'd had a long day, and so, since they'd be rising with the chickens to travel on, he headed on up to his own flop. Longarm didn't really give a shit about charting uncharted wilderness they wouldn't be riding through for days to come. So he excused himself and left the army men to work things out if he was correct in assuming they had eyes for those strange gals mixed in with other passengers still sharing the smoke-filled lobby.

Longarm knew, as no doubt both army men knew, how some passengers traveling on a limited budget skipped meals and sat up at overnight transfer stops unless they met up with fellow travelers willing to treat. In theory, sharing a Pullman berth or hotel room with a fellow traveler wasn't the same as paying a whore. But Longarm found it hard to make the distinction, and that had been another reason to send poor fat Kitty back to Saint Lou so pure.

Since he could afford to, Longarm undressed in one of the dinky cheek-by-jowl rooms upstairs and flopped bare-ass on the lumpy mattress before it occured to him he'd surely have one of those tedious dreams if he didn't take a good leak before he fell asleep.

He rolled out of bed and knelt to explore under the bed for the chamber pot he certainly hoped he'd find. But he didn't. Some small town hotels short on hired help could be that mean. They saved on wages by letting the guests take care of their own body wastes.

It hurt to get dressed some more and head down the hall to their pisser, but he knew it was that or one of those endless dreams where you keep seeking a place to piss, only somebody always comes along to stare and you have to dash on in hopes of finding a better place and so on until you wake up to just—damnit—piss and get it over with.

So once he got it over with, Longarm padded back along the hall on bare feet, bemused to hear snoring so early through one door he passed.

Then he heard dirtier noises coming through another door and would have passed on had he not recognized the voice of Wilma Thalmann as she pleaded, "Deeper, darling! Up my ass as far as you can go!"

So that seemed to account for the hold she had on old Agent Thalmann, until he heard Pecos Moran growl in a lower tone, "Not so loud, little darling! You want the whole fucking hotel to know I'm fucking you in the ass, you wild and crazy gal?"

Longarm moved on, grinning like a disgusted fox in a henhouse full of spoiled poultry, as he marveled at the ways of a mind as dirty as hers had to be. It was up for grabs who she'd try to get into a fight with her new conquest. But what the hell. Moran wouldn't be with them past Animas Point, and Billy Vail's orders were to ride on through as sudden as possible.

He got back to his own hired cubicle, and almost gasped aloud when he opened the door to see somebody standing there in the faint light from the dimly lit hallway and the window on the shadowy outline's far side.

Then he recognized the voice of Sister Marsha Olan as she soberly said, "Buck . . . we have to talk."

Chapter 9

Longarm said he was all ears as he stepped inside and shut the hall door after him. The first thing he learned before she'd said another word was that she seemed to be standing shorter, now, even though he was standing barefoot. So she wasn't wearing her high buttons and seemed to have on a dark bathrobe. She'd let her ash blond hair down and it was too early to say what she might or might not have on under the robe as she said, "I can't go on. I won't go on. That crazy woman is bound and determined to get someone killed, and it's not going to be *me*! They don't pay me that much! I signed on for adventure and a change of scene, but I'm a highly-trained professional and there's more than one fine hospital will have me, right in the District of Columbia. Why don't we both stay here in Del Rio and explore the local sights together before we catch that night run back to Denver, Buck?"

He took her by one hand and sat her on the bed as he told her she had not the least notion how tempting her offer sounded. But as he sat down beside her, he said, "The expedition needs us both. Them mysterious unregistered Indians needs us both, Miss Marsha. It was you telling me, back in Denver, how awful kids looked, dying of smallpox! I thought the four of us had agreed abaord that train that Miss Wilma was about out of ammunition."

Marsha sobbed, "That was then, and now she'd bedded down with that Texas Ranger, hatching up more devilment! She started out to seduce him the moment he joined our party here in Del Rio, and I, for one, was hardly surprised to see she'd succeeded!"

Longarm smiled wryly to reply, "Nor I. He's a man, and she's a fine-looking woman. Don't let this get around, but most men are ever ready to be seduced by uglier gals by far. We have no shame in such matters and ought to be whipped with snakes, dad blast our horny souls!"

She replied with a soft bitter laugh, "You forget I've studied medicine and . . . reproductive anatomy. I'm not trying to act like a blushing virgin, Buck. I have my own anatomy and . . . feelings. But I don't think Wilma Thalmann gets a thing out of cheating on her husband but the evil chuckles of skating on thin ice! Tonight's not the first time, and that Texas Ranger's not the first total stranger she's made love to, almost within earshot of her husband's bed, on our way out here from the district. One was a young bellhop during our layover in New York. She as much as dared poor Fiona and me to betray her lewd behavior with our Pullman porter aboard the New York Central, and we were both sure that poor colored boy was as shocked by her lovemaking as we were, judging by his muffled protests through a compartment door. You see, she doesn't settle for . . . the old-fashioned way."

Longarm murmured, "I noticed, passing Moran's door just now. I ain't one for telling tales out of school, Miss Marsha, but it may settle your nerves to hear the lady told me, earlier, her husband knows and doesn't care, or doesn't seem man enough to do anything about the ways she carries on so extra *muros* ad nauseam."

The trained nurse laughed incredulously and gasped, "*Et tu, Brute*? They made us study Latin at nursing school, and how did you resist her when she made a pass at *you*?"

Longarm shrugged and confessed, *"Nolo contendere.* I reckon I'm a sissy when it comes to *amor proximi ad absurdum."*

She laughed and asked where he'd been required to study Latin. So he kicked himself mentally for the slip as he spun her some bullshit about typing up court transcripts. For it would have been just as easy to tell her he didn't carry love one's neighbor to the point of dumb without showing off the baby-talk Latin all lawmen were exposed to.

She was too worried about Wilma Thalmann's troublemaking to follow up on the past of "Buck Crawford." So it was easy to steer her back on that track. But she still said she wasn't going on with the rest of them in the morning and seemed to have that hand resting on his denim clad thigh as she pleaded with him to stay behind with her.

He sighed and said, "I'd sure like to, Sister Marsha, even if you were an ugly boy. But the government of these United States is counting on me to guide them down through the canyon lands to Fort Defiance at the least. They might or might not find canyon land scouts there to lead them further into unmapped bewilderment. But I got to get 'em at least that far, and you know the way back to Denver without me, and even if I rode that far with you, we'd have to part company there, unless I got fired for deserting the Thalmann's and had no place particular to be. So you see how it's got to be, and I sure wish I could get you to go on down to Fort Defiance with us because, to tell the truth, I'll miss you like fire if you don't!"

So the next thing he knew, she'd half-risen to fork one thigh over his and sit astride his lap as she hugged him hard and kissed him in a far from sisterly fashion. So, seeing he found nothing but smooth warm hide under that robe, he responded in kind, falling backwards across the lumpy mattress with her on top and a knee hugging his ribs to either side. He felt obliged to point out, even as she was fumbling at his pants, "I'd be lying if I asked you to stop! But this ain't the way anyone gets me to quit before I'm fired!"

She murmured with her lips pressed to his, "I know, you gallant fool! Do you think I'd be this forward if I thought I had weeks on the trail ahead to let *you* make the first move?"

Seeing no sensible reason to set further conditions on whatever the hell they were doing, Longarm rolled her off so's he could shuck the gun belt, shirt and jeans he'd slipped into just to take a piss. By the time he had, her robe had opened wide to expose all she had to offer a man as if she was a Delmonico blue point on the half-shell. So he helped himself to what she so freely offered, and, as he entered her, they both gasped in surprised delight at the just-right fit of what she'd described as re-productive anatomy.

Her tits were swell, too, albeit smaller and firmer than those of the dusky Cecila Mandalian, way back when. As if to make up for that, Marsha's pale willowy curves *felt* softer whilst *looking* firmer in the moonglow through the grimy window near the head of the bed.

As if by silent agreement, they made love more tenderly than the overactive Cecilia had wanted it, and that felt novel, too. So once they got to really hot but sweet with a pillow under her ass, and her long legs wrapped around his waist, Longarm almost blurted out how grand it was that no matter how many women a man might bed in an average lifetime, he was never going to run out of new thrills unless or until he did it with the same gal 'til it commenced to feel like *work* after those magic dozens of times it was worth it, if they were any good at all.

The less said about that the better, and, as a kindly old philosopher had once remarked, no doubt in French, even should as many as one out of ten turn out bad, a man could still enjoy the experience for the novelty.

He suspected from pillow conversation as they shared a second-wind cheroot that Sister Marsha might have simular views on novelty. She never asked him where he'd learned to screw so considerate, and he was far too considerate to inquire where she'd learned to screw so sweet. She'd *said* she'd studied anatomy and didn't want him to take her for any blushing virgin. They smoked and talked a spell before they agreed it was dumb to try to change one another's minds. She wasn't going on with the rest of them in the morning, and he wasn't going back to Denver with her, no matter what she said or did. So they snuffed out the cheroot and just got really down and dirty for the sheer pleasure of a healthy man and woman meeting as ships in the night. It was grand but well short of midnight when she kissed him with wet cheeks and whispered she had to go.

He didn't ask how come. He'd been fighting not to plead and beg for her to come along, come morning. It was best for ships passing in the night to just sail on and say no more about it.

He didn't ask questions when he failed to see her at breakfast with the others. Nobody asked him where she might be, and that seemed a good way to leave things.

But after they boarded the westbound for the morning run over to Durango, Longarm found himself seated with Doc Frank and Sister Fiona some more and the doc told him he'd found a note from Marsha shoved under his door back in Del Rio.

Frank said, "She tells us she had to go back to D.C. because of a family emergency. I wonder which family she was worried about? I can't see how she'd have heard about events back home after supper, last night, can you?"

Longarm shrugged and pointed out there'd been a Western Union in Del Rio. He said *he'd* sent a wire to Denver from there. Nobody asked why, and he had no call to say he'd be picking up any answers his aunt sent back when he got to the Western Union in Durango.

He didn't ask whether the doc had shown the note to the Thalmanns. They'd have been looking for Marsha earlier if Frank hadn't. Unless you wanted everyone to know all about your private life, you didn't ask needless questions about others.

Doc Frank said he hoped to borrow an army nurse from Fort Defiance, since there wouldn't be time to recruit another civilian Sister in Durango. Longarm didn't care. He found himself trying not to stare at the far end of the car, where Pecos Moran lounged brazen in his seat facing the woman he'd been sodomizing and her understanding husband, Agent Thalmann.

Young Lieutenant Grover was trying to start up with a plain-faced farm gal with a great shape. Sergeant Wynn seemed to be doing better with an older gal with a heroic ass under her polka-dot summer frock. It sure beat all how dumb men seemed to act around women, unless you were one of them your own self. He idly wondered whether old Wilma's man-hungry feelings had a lot to do with her drive to spoil such fun for others. He was trying to recall the name of that hell-fire-and-damnation preacher man who'd been caught at it with the whole choir in a bare-ass Roman orgy in the organ loft.

He knew Doc Frank had been talking to Agent Thalmann about other matters when the sawbones said they were being met at the end of the line by a contract trail boss and some Indian hands from the South Ute Reserve. Frank said, "Thalmann seems anxious to move out in such daylight as we have to work with this afternoon. We've been told not to worry about water or campsites as long as we're following the Animas south from Durango. But south of the jump-off at Animas Point I find the map *meshuggah*! The pony trails wander over the map like they were laid out by a blind drunk, and why are we making for Fort Defiance *south* of Canyon de Chelly when those lost Chindi are supposed to be hidden in some unmapped canyon *between* those two landmarks? So won't that mean we'll go south of Canyon de Chelly to hairpin back to the north again?"

Longarm nodded and explained, "Where the country ain't mapped, you follow such trails as game critters, Mister Lo, the poor Indian, and just possibly some luckier prospectors have blazed ahead of you. The long way around on a paper chart can be the *only* way one can make it across the high, dry country. Making it from one water hole to the next without falling into the pumpkin makes more sense than beelines through such treacherous terrain."

Sister Fiona stared copper-penny, wide-eyed across at him to ask in a puzzled tone, "Falling into pumpkins, Buck?"

He said, "Indian notion that describes the lay of the canyon lands better than some others. So far, we've got most of the big canyons and mayhaps a tenth of the smaller-side canyons mapped, with hardly one of the *really* small side canyons branching twisty, a few yards wide and a mile or so deep. When you're down in one such a water-carved cleft in the orange Navaho sandstone the Colorado Plateau rides atop, the sunlight leaking down through the water-polished cliffs makes 'em sort of look as if you were a bug wandering about inside a big ripe pumpkin. That can be dangerous enough. When you ride across the flat mesa lands unwary, you can spy a yards-wide slot ahead and literally fall into the pumpkin for a mile or more, bouncing back and forth betwixt solid rock that only *looks* like hollowed-out pumpkin."

The chestnut-haired Sister with copper penny eyes

asked why it was dangerous to be down in the pumpkin if you didn't fall in. She sure was one for questions, considering.

Longarm explained, "Flash flooding. The Four Corners country is rightly classified as semiarid but the *weather* ain't hot and dry as the thirsty land's deep and rapid drainage. Winter brings snow in high places that melts predictable all summer to feed the better known river canyons. This late summer weather inspires smaller scattered thunderstorms, leaving clear blue skies above some canyons about to flood from a gullywasher thirty or forty miles away, with the water traveling thirty miles an hour or more. Get caught in one of the wider canyons by a ten-foot wall of brown froth and you just might see a way to climb above it. Meet the same flash flood in a yards-wide cleft and bits and pieces of you may or may not be found a long, long ways downstream, by critters. Nobody ever *searches* for the remains of travelers lost in the canyon lands. Wouldn't do anybody any good if they did. So they don't. Albeit now and again an Indian or a wandering prospector might show up with a watch, a gun or even a hat for sale."

Doc Frank said, "Remind me never to fall in any pumpkins with my hat. You're trying to tell us we have to zig, zag and ziggle some more from one safe place to another in unsafe surroundings, right?"

Longarm said that was about the size of it and excused himself to step out on the platform for a smoke. Explaining the obvious to dudes before you got to simply point details out got tedious, and little Sister Fiona had been staring at him funny, as if wanting to ask him something like where ladies shit on open desert in broad daylight.

As he lit up on the platform he saw they were making good time down the western slope of the continental divide, with the scenery getting flatter and more open, now. So he was in a fair mood when Sister Fiona came out to

join him. But he could see she felt awkward as all g..
out as he nodded and commented on how much faster
they were moving, now.

To which she replied with her copper penny eyes
mighty worried, "Buck, I have to know. Is it true you
raped Marsha Olan back in Del Rio? Is it true that's why
she couldn't go on to Durango with the rest of us, lest
you rape her again?"

Chapter 10

It was tempting. It would have been easy. But Longarm refused to stoop to the same dirty game of tittle-tattle. He simply asked the wide-eyed Fiona if they hadn't agreed to present a united front against Wilma Thalmann's nasty mouth.

Fiona insisted, "Where there's smoke, there's fire, and more than one old beau has said I wasn't as dumb as I looked. So I could tell Marsha fancied you, and now she's gone, so there!"

Longarm blew smoke the other way as he nodded, then pointed out a man had no call to rape anyone who fancied him. He let that sink in before he added, "I don't even tell *true* tales out of school as a rule, but since you haven't asked yourself why a gal who fancied any member of this expedition would want to *leave* the same, I can tell you Marsha was afraid with good reason that Agent Thalmann is a stuck-up fool with a stuck-up troublemaker for a wife. Didn't she tell *you* they just weren't paying you ladies enough to hunt snipe in dangerous country with incompetents spoiling for disaster?"

Fiona replied, "She did utter words to that effect, now that you remind me. But I don't have her experience, and

I need the job. What's your excuse, Buck?"

Longarm said she'd just given it and suggested she go back inside before Wilma Thalmann decided he was raping her.

Fiona batted her copper penny eyes and said none of her old beaus had ever had to resort to such desperate measures. Then she turned to flounce inside as Longarm murmured, "Well, well, well, but what in thunder would we talk about, afterwards?"

He finished his smoke, went back inside, and when Lieutenant Grover signaled from the middle of the car, Longarm went forth to join the two army engineers over the survey chart they'd spread on the empty seat facing theirs.

Grover said, "We've been going over the wagon trace running down from Durango to Fort Defiance. Say we manage as much as twenty-five miles a day in the saddle . . ."

"We won't," Longarm cut in, explaining, "Cavalry on open prairie averages twenty to thirty miles a day on mortal horseflesh it has to rest and water along the way. The semiarid canyon lands are rougher on horseflesh and all that baggage you-all brought with you from the district will be a drop in the bucket to the trail gear waiting for us at the end of these rails. The pack train loaned by the South Ute agency will be loaded down with everything from tents to tons, not pounds, of food and fodder. Ain't enough natural greenery down yonder to graze as you go. You have to pack cracked corn for each and every horse or mule in the train and, pound for pound, a horse or mule puts away more by the day than we do."

The young shavetail sighed and said, "They taught us all that at the Point, Buck. Sergeant Wynn and me have been questioning all the zigs and zags. As this trail to Fort Defiance is laid out, it could take us forever to get there!"

"More like the better part of three weeks," Longarm

suggested as he drew a straight line across the chart to point out, "Hundred and thirty miles by crow. Thrice as far along a wagon trace laid out as short as practical where you have to go around mile-deep holes in the ground from one water hole to the next, with water holes up to eighty miles apart, and the water you're packing eight pounds to a gallon. Make the practical route an even four hundred miles to save calculating fractions and say we can manage fifteen or better a day."

The academy-trained engineer said, "Twenty days to Fort Defiance and then we double back, how far, to that fucking canyon full of Chindi Indians?"

Longarm shrugged and said, "If there's any such place. I could tell you a tale of Spaniards searching for the Seven Cities of Cibola on the Colorado Plateau, but you gents look worried enough. It was my understanding it was up to *you* to put such a canyon on the map, if we ever find it."

Seeing that hadn't cheered either worth mention, Longarm went back to sit with Doc Frank and Sister Fiona. Nothing he could say made *them* feel any better either as the scenery outside got flatter and drier.

They rolled into Durango before noon. Durango, whether in reference to Durango, Colorado, or the bigger Durango down Mexico way, still meant something like a tough corner, and that fit the freshly-sprouted mushroom by the *Rio de las Animas Perdidas* or "River of the Lost Souls." Rough and ready railroaders and nesters just called it the Animas.

Everything about Durango was still rough and ready. The township's incorporation papers hadn't been approved in Denver yet, and the finer railroad terminal meant to serve the broad guage they were laying to replace the ad hoc narrow guage was a work still in progress. Once they got it all put together, Durango was to serve as a rail hub serving smaller mining camps in all directions. There were no mines in the mushroom's patch of the Animas valley but hog farms and cow spreads were sprouting all about to feed a projected population of over a thousand, Lord willing, if the mines didn't bottom out west of the divide.

They were met on the platform by an Indian with a wrinkled apple face in a fancy charro riding outfit, along with the denim clad and longer haired Utes he'd brought along to handle their baggage. He spoke good English and told them to call him Tosawi. He said he had the two dozen ponies and heavier camp gear in a corral just up the northsouth Main Avenue in line with the narrow guage down from the Silverton strike. His silent helpers picked up the baggage Longarm and all the other men but Agent Thalmann had unloaded from their train, and as they all started walking, Longarm fell in beside the crusty-looking older man to try his own limited grasp of Ho Hada on Tosawi. Most Indians seemed to appreciate the gesture.

Towasi didn't turn out like most Indians. He snorted in disgust and said, "Don't be such an asshole, *tabebo*! Have I been speaking babytalk in your tongue? I don't see why you people think we give a shit when you learn to say *ae* or *ka* to us? Do you think we are dogs to be to be taught yes or no? Hear me, when you want one of my young men to do something you will tell me what it is, and I will tell him to do it, if I think he should. Don't expect any of us to shine boots or empty chamber pots. We have agreed to get your *taibo* down to Fort Defiance alive. That is all. We will get along better on the trail if you don't try to fuck with us. I have spoken."

Longarm nodded amiably and said, "I follow your drift, chief. If it's any comfort I never voted for Governor Pitkin back in '76."

Tosawi shrugged and kept walking as he said, "I was never *kikmonkwi*. All out chiefs are in prison or living apart from us on rich food and firewater so they vote the

88

way the B.I.A. wants them to vote. If your money grub-bing Fred Pitkin wasn't the governor, the mine owners would have chosen another who hated us just as much. Hear me, I rode with Rope Thrower Carson. I scouted for the Gray Wolf Crook. Nobody I have ever ridden with had any part in the trouble up on the White River. But now I am lower than a black *taibo* in the eyes of you white *taibo*. You let the blacks you look down on run free. We are watched over like unruly children. Hear me, we don't like it. Hear me, we would fight you if we had a chance. But we know we don't have a chance, and so we have to put up with your bullshit if we want our women and children to be fed!"

Longarm said, "Well, I tried, so fuck you, and I got to run over to the Western Union, now. Leave my saddle and a pony at that corral if you leave without me."

He'd been to Durango before, so he had no call to ask directions through the hustle and bustle and kicked-up dust of a new settlement in the making. At the telegraph office on Railroad Avenue he found a terse but encoded day-rates wire from his aunt in Denver, confirming there was really a Texas Ranger named James or Pecos Moran and that another informant had come forward to say he'd seen the late Tiburcio Vasquez, a rampaging California road agent of Hispanic persuasion, at the bar in Madam Marlotte's whorehouse in Animas Point.

This only sounded reasonable until one recalled the public hanging of Tiburcio in Sacramento, back in '75.

Putting the wire away, Longarm paused on the board-walk out front to light a cheroot as he decided, "All right, one mean-looking Mex could be mistaken for another. Or somebody could be making live men up to look like dead men hiding out in that whorehouse. But how come? If it's a con game, what's the pitch? If it's all a big joke, what's the point, and where's the humor?"

A familiar figure in black denim and ten gallons worth

of hat joined him out front of the Western Union to observe, "Great minds run in the same channels. I got to wire my home office and let 'em know I've throwed in with you B.I.A. riders at least as far south as Animas Point. We ain't leaving before three. Miss Wilma wants to shop for some fancier rations than them Indians brought, and the mean one says we can make the nearby Ute Agency in four or five hours. Seems we get to lay over, there, and ride on with fresh ponies far as where I part company with you-all at Animas Point. Old Tosawi says he'll swap agency ponies for fresh ones at Animas Point. Sure seems to be one horse-swapping redskin!"

Longarm said, "I didn't cotton to him, neither. But we both know the country ahead in antler-shedding time, or August, as our calendar describes the same. Go ahead and send your wire. I'll wait out here and walk back with you."

So that was how they worked it out as Longarm debated with himself whether to bring the other lawman up to date on that rumor about the long dead Tiburcio Vasquez. In the end, he recalled Billy Vail's orders not to even let the law in Animas Point in on his mission, and Vail's caution made sense. They were sending him the long way in, undercover, because whenever known lawmen rode within miles of that mysterious whorehouse in a small dusty trail town, all those spooks seemed to vanish into the literally thin, dry air.

To date, those repeated rumors of highly-prized outlaws had attracted other lawmen and not-as-lawsome bounty hunters to search the premises and pat down the less mysterious whores and customers who seemed to replace the spooks the moment a lawman appeared. Vail's notion was you had to be a lawless-looking cuss, like more than one of their paid informants. This required Longarm to drift in alone, and if the spooks of the haunted whorehouse followed their usual rote, the ranger would be long gone by the time a dusty, recently-fired saddle tramp rode in out of the canyon lands to the southwest.

When Moran rejoined him, it was quarter to two. So they had time for the last drink they'd be fixing to order for a spell and decided the Elkhead Saloon on Main Avenue would do. As they bellied up to the bar, the Texan observed he was just as glad he wouldn't be riding on past Animas Point with the cantankerous Tosawi and his sullen young Utes. He said, "Texas will be content with me explaining all them dead outlaws playing slap and tickle in a whorehouse overlooking the River of the Lost Souls. Do you reckon there could be a connection?"

Longarm wasn't supposed to be a lawman who knew about the haunted whorehouse ahead. So he made Moran fill him in on the mystery, and confirm that Billy Vail hadn't been the only distant lawman who'd been sold the wild yarn.

Once it seemed safe for him to offer an opinion without tipping his own hand, Longarm suggested, "What if it's some sort of tourist attraction, like the Cardiff Giant or that pickled head of Joaquin Murieta you can pay to see in Frisco? I have it on good authority the Cardiff Giants, plural, are both crudely-fashioned statues, and there never was a single Mex bandit named Joaquin Murieta."

Moran asked why anyone would go to the trouble of faking a haunted whorehouse in a remote trail town.

Longarm paid for the first round as he replied, "I don't know. It makes more sense, or at least it seems more possible, to haunt any sort of house with actors made up to resemble well-known dead folk than it does to imagine a whorehouse full of real haunts, though."

Moran said he'd drink to that. So they clinked beer schooners and inhaled some suds before the Texan sighed and said, "Maybe I'd feel better riding on with you-all and them uppity Indians, after all, if only I could. At least there's nothing *mysterious* about old Tosawi. He's just an ornery old bastard."

Longarm said, "I'll drink to *that*, and I mean to have a word about him when we get to the South Ute Agency. For a man who's found a home with the B.I.A. most horse Indians would lend you a wife for, he's carrying on meaner than recent Indian policy justifies. For unlike the *North* Utes, who really had just cause to be pissed with the late Nate Meeker, Tosawi's *South* Utes have been neither punished nor dispossessed for some mighty foolish rape and slaughter."

"I thought you just said them North Ute were justified," said Moran.

Longarm shook his head and explained, "They were justified when they protested arrogant stupidity on the part of their agent on the White River reserve. Nate Meeker made them plant corn and truck that just wouldn't ripen way up in the middle of the air. And he had his white help plow a sage flat the Indians had been using as a racetrack. When they complained, he cut off their rations and wired the army they'd been setting forest fires and burning out white settlers who weren't supposed to be on land reserved for Indians in the first place. But it was twice as stupid and mean-hearted for the Indians to shoot down Meeker and seven other white B.I.A. men, along with a field grade officer and some cavalry troopers they ambushed shortly after."

Longarm sipped more suds and added, "Carrying off three weeping white women to pass around with other luxuries looted from the White River trading post played right into the hands of mining and rangeland speculators who'd never cottoned to that much Indian reserve on the west side of the divide to begin with. We wouldn't be standing here in this new town had not the Indians, themselves, offered such a fine excuse to run 'em off and open the whole west slope to white settlement."

He sipped more suds, belched, and added, "Tosawi knows that, since he speaks perfect English and likely reads the newspapers. Meanwhile, he's a horse Indian and self-confessed government scout who's still being paid to handle horses for the U.S. Government. So, seeing I'm the trail boss assigned to the expedition by the government in question, me and old Tosawi seem headed for a showdown in the not-too-distant future!"

Chapter 11

At that corral on Main Avenue, they found the imperious
Wilma had taken the five Indians with her to fetch and
carry, leaving the others waiting amid or atop their own
baggage and the tonnage gathered by Tosawi in the shade
of a sage-thatched ramada alongside the pole corral, where
three dozen Indian ponies with B.I.A. brands had been
fenced apart from a dozen-odd livery nags. Longarm nodded with approval as he saw how many of the Indian stock
seemed at least part Barb. The Ho Hada called Ute had
gotten into the riding and raising of horseflesh shorty after
their pioneering cousins, the Comanche, who'd stolen the
first Spanish horses back in the 1600s. And, considering
they were less famous horse Indians than say Lakota,
thanks to their highland hunting grounds where no buffalo
roamed, the Ute had been horse-riding sons of bitches in
their shining times.

The late Agent Meeker had lost track of that, or hadn't
cared, when he'd tried to make them give up their pony
herds in favor of high and dry farming where a Swiss
could see the land was best for grazing stock.

Longarm hefted his own borrowed roping saddle and
draped it handy over a corral pole as Agent Thalmann

hailed him. He ambled over to the cuss, idly wondering what he had stuck crosswise up his ass this time, judging from the expression on his pickle puss.

Thalmann wasted no time asking, "Are you in some sort of trouble with the law, Crawford? I've a right to know before we head out into open desert with you, dammit!"

Longarm truthfully replied, when you studied on it, "I can give you my word I ain't in trouble with the law. What makes you suspect I could be?"

Thalmann said, "My wife tells me that ranger, yonder, has been asking questions about you, for one thing. More recently, within this very hour, a local who said he worked for a newspaper came by to ask how long I'd known you. Said he'd seen you before in these parts but didn't recall them calling you Buck Crawford."

Longarm managed a poker face as he asked, "Did he say what name he might know me by, or the name of the paper he says he works for?"

"I didn't think to ask either question," Thalmann replied with a mortified expression, adding, "My wife tells me Ranger Moran suspects you're not exactly what you seem, too!"

To which Longarm dryly replied, "Reckon they have to find something to talk about, between times. I'll ask him if he aims to arrest me before we leave town."

But as he started to turn away Agent Thalmann gasped, "No, don't! He'll know Wilma told us!"

"Wouldn't want anyone to hear Miss Wilma confides in her husband!" Longarm muttered, turning away in mingled amusement and concern as he wondered whether it might be time to cut the ranger in on things.

By the time he'd made it back to his borrowed saddle to draw the Winchester '73 from its boot and load the magazine he'd of course left empty during its train ride as tossed-about baggage, Pecos Moran rejoined him to ask what was up.

Deciding not to confide too much in a man who confided in a bitch like old Wilma, Longarm told the ranger, "Some bird who says he's a newspaperman has been asking questions about me. Reckon he thinks I might be one of them spirit mediums, headed for Animas Point to hold a seance in that mysterious whorehouse."

"Did he ask about *me*?" the ranger inquired.

Longarm shrugged and said, "If he did, Thalmann never said so. Why don't you ask him your own self?"

Moran strode away to do just that as Longarm marveled at the gall of a man who'd fuck a man's wife in the ass and walk bare-faced up to him with a hand held out friendly.

Longarm didn't consider himself prim and proper. There were heaps of tribal customs and even statute laws he was inclined to ignore. But being two-faced when he didn't have to be two-faced wasn't one of 'em, and it was way easier to keep your hands off a married woman than it was to indulge in an unfunny bedroom farce just for a piece of ass no better than any other to be had at far less risk to a good or bad marriage, to say nothing of your own ass!

Sister Fiona, who hadn't been invited along on Wilma Thalmann's last minute shopping trip, came over to ask when they'd be leaving.

He laughed and said, "It don't seem up to me. But they told me *three*, and it's well after two, Ma'am."

She dimpled up at him to say, "I don't mind you calling me Fiona if I can call you Buck. I've been thinking about what Miss Wilma said about you and poor scared Marsha. It was awfully mean of Miss Wilma to say, even if there was anything to it."

Longarm slid the last round of .44-40 into the magazine and slid the Winchester back in its boot with the chamber empty as he just let that simmer in her mind without answering it. As a lawman well versed in questioning suspects, he knew the less you said in your own defense, the less likely you were to make one of those fatal slips a canny questioner was waiting on.

Folk with things to hide hardly ever blurted right out that they had done the deed. A savvy questioner got them to throwing bullshit fast and furious, hoping they'd slip up and let fly with a detail only a guilty party had call to know. He knew Fiona, being a woman, was curious about what had really taken place back in Del Rio, and he, being a man, had to resist the impulse to brag on his winnings.

Fiona threw him a curve by observing with no advance warning that Tosawi, that mean old Ute, didn't seem to like him, either.

She said, "When I told him you'd explained to us about having to beeline between water holes on the way to Fort Defiance, he called you a dreadful name and said you didn't know anything about the trail to Fort Defiance. Do the two of you know one another from an earlier time out this way?"

Longarm said, "He thinks he knows me. Colonel Carson tried to get his Ute scouts a better deal from Washington. But to them they were betrayed by Rope Thrower, a squaw man who spoke their lingo and knew their ways. They used to have friendlier words for us. But now we're all the same *taibo* to them, a term as friendly as say Dago or Kike. I'd as soon not tell a lady how *tabebo* translates. But he'd kill his version of the golden goose if he agreed to trail boss us through to Fort Defiance and dropped us into the pumpkin instead."

She nodded but said, "I thought they said *you* were going to be our guide and trail boss, Buck."

He smiled thinly and said, "So did I. That may be one of the things old Tosawi is upset about. But I ain't out to steal his thunder. They only sent me along as a sort of spare, in case nobody else could find the way to Fort Defiance and that uncharted tribe the rest of you are out to register and vaccinate. I'll have a word with Tosawi once we've rid together a ways."

So later that evening he did, but first Wilma Thalmann had to get back with the four young bucks loaded down with groceries and sour-faced Tosawi looking worse.

It was after three, of course, and it took time to saddle the stock with A-frame packs and Indian riding saddles as well as the two sidesaddles, four army saddles and battered stock saddle off the D & RGRR. So they barely cleared the south side of Durango by four, with the August sun more than halfway down the western half of the cobalt blue bowl of cloudless sky. So the trail was hot and dusty as it got in the moon-of-shedding-antlers out yonder.

But as Wilma had sniffed when her husband gently chided her for the late start, they were only a stage run from the agency compound they meant to shelter at, their first night out.

This was true and had they been traveling by stagecoach they'd have made the eighteen miles or less in time for supper. But whilst coach lines managed nine miles an hour along their routes, changing teams every eighteen miles or less to go on behind fresh mules at a mile-eating trot, getting there the old-fashioned way with loaded down horseflesh took longer. A horse ran or trotted way faster than a man on foot and walked a tad slower. Unless it rested a spell at least every other hour it didn't walk as far. So an average speed of three miles an hour was asking about as much as you had a right to expect from a pack pony, and there was no point in having pack ponies if you meant to lope on ahead of 'em.

And so it came to pass that they still had a ways to ride when the cloudless sunset and the first wishing star in the purple sky to the east caught them watering and resting their ponies along the Animas.

99

When Wilma Thalmann naturally bitched about that, it was old Tosawi who declared, "Hear me! I told you back in Durango we would hear the owl on the trail if you kept buying fish eggs and laughing water. Now we are too far from the agency to make it before dark and too close to bother making camp. We will change your saddles to fresh ponies and then I will run a line through all your bridles to keep you all from straying like chickens from the river trail. I have spoken!"

He doubtless thought he had, but when he joined Longarm with a rope end as the taller white man was saddling a paint mare with his borrowed roper, Longarm told him, "I ain't a chicken. I'd as soon go my own way along the trail, no offense."

Tosawi said, "Hear me, you will do as I say because I am the trail boss, here, not you!"

Longarm lowered his voice to reply firmly but not unkindly, "We'd best have that out here and now, in private lest I make you look like a woman who rides sidesaddle in front of the others."

The older man reared like a challenged herd stallion to snap. "You think you can make me look like a woman? Hear me! I am not afraid to fight you! You are bigger than me. You are younger than me, but you can't be *braver* than me, and I count coup on *Apache* as well as Navaho and Arapaho, Cheyenne and Sioux!"

"Those were the days," Longarm nodded, adding, "I don't want to fight you. It would not be a good fight, no matter who won. I could count coup on *Ho Hada* if I thought old grudges mattered that much. I don't think they do, and we don't have to fight to settle who might be the boss here."

Tosawi bitterly demanded, "You think you have to be the boss because you are *taibo*?"

Longarm said, "Nope, I agree the *taibo* couple in command of this B.I.A. show need help finding their way to the

100

shithouse. Let's just say I have *puha* I can call upon if I have to, and then don't make me have to. I don't care who the others call the trail boss. I won't counter your orders as long as they ain't aimed at making me look like a big baby who can't ride worth shit. I won't do anything to make you look bad as long as it's understood that should you force my hand I have the *puha* to run you clean the fuck out of Colorado to live on flour and beans on that Uinita Ouray Reserve in the badlands of the Utah Territory, with other mule-headed Ho who can't seem to get along with us *saltu*, not *taibo*, who mean them no harm!"

Longarm was braced for a blow. The old Indian looked as if he might be fixing to throw one, then Tosawi nodded soberly, his wrinkled face unreadable in the gathering dusk, to decide, "I think I know who you are. I have heard of a *taibo*, all right, a *saltu ka saltu* who put an agent at the Uinita ouray agency in prison for cheating Ho Hada out of rations so he could sell them in Salt Lake City. They say this *saltu ka saltu* does not try to soften real people up with soft words. They say that when he thinks you are a sister fucker he *calls* you a sister fucker. If you are this stranger who is not a stranger, we might be able to get along after all."

Longarm said, "Let's just get along and not worry about who I really am. I have reasons for not talking too much about myself. I can tell you I have not come to do any harm to Ho Hada. That is all I wish to say."

Tosawi said, "Hear me. That is enough. I will not ask who you are or what you are doing here, and you will not use your *puha* with the B.I.A. against me. Have we spoken?"

"We have spoken," said Longarm. So they shook on it.

An hour later, riding alongside the strung together dudes on his own free ranging paint, Longarm heard a frightened gasp and reined in alongside Fiona to ask the chestnut-haired little thing what was eating her.

Pointing up at the cloudless sky, bespangled at that altitude with way more stars than one saw back in the District of Columbia, Fiona said, "I keep seeing falling stars and, oh, look! There falls another one! What's going on up there, Buck?"

He said, "August. There are other such showers in the spring and early winter, but this is the time of the year you see the most such falling stars. Pawnee hold falling stars to be a good sign. Apache and Navaho are scared of 'em. You ain't scared of bitty falling stars, are you, Fiona?"

She decided, "Not if you say it's safe to ride along under them. The skies are pretty out this way, once you get used to how *big* they seem. What did you say to that mean old Indian back there? He seems to like you better, now."

Longarm said, "You just have to know how to talk to Indians, I reckon. Tosawi's all right, just uncertain how to act around our kind. So he puts on a brave front lest we suspect he's uneasy in our company."

She brightened and said, "Oh, I had a dancing master like that one time, back East. My mother thought I ought to take lessons so she enrolled me in his class, and he was ever so strict and mean to me until one afternoon when we were alone in the studio he just up and threw me down on the floor and tried to take my pantaloons off!"

Longarm gravely replied he'd heard some strict teachers were like that. She said, "I never saw him after that. When I screamed, he jumped off me and ran out, yelling something about my driving him mad, mad, mad, and when I got home and told my mother about it she said I'd had enough dancing lessons and enrolled me in a nursing school instead. Some of the teachers *there* were awfully mean and strict with me, too. I wish I had your way of making friends with mean, strict people!"

To which Longarm could only reply, "Like I said, you just have to know how to talk to 'em."

Chapter 12

Considering all their twaddle about bloodthirsty fiends and noble savages, a heap of reporters who wrote about Mister Lo, the poor Indian, had not the least notion what an Indian reservation was or how one worked.

Like others, the South Ute reserve astraddle the Animas and other northsouth rivers such as the Plata and Piños was not a prison for Indians. There was no fence around better than a thousand square miles of mixed mountain and high desert traditional hunting grounds. The word reservation means the land was reserved for the tribe so named, off-limits to white settlers claiming government lands under the Homestead Act of 1862 unless and until said Indians offered an excuse for ever-ready land grabbers to evict them.

That happened more to some nations than to others. The Taos pueblo off to the east was the oldest inhabited town in the United States because once the live-and-let-live Pueblos had taught the old-time Spaniards not to push 'em too far, they'd managed to get along with first old Mexico and then New Mexico, offering no excuses for anyone to move 'em off their traditional holdings. Their Apache enemies, *Apache* meaning "enemy" in Pueblo, offered grim examples of another approach to red and white relationships, with their repeated so-called "reservation jumps"—not escapes from some sort of prison camp but bare-faced raiding expeditions for fun and profit, off their own reservation for the same reason Robin Hood had robbed the rich in the old country. Neither other Apache nor poor folk had much worth taking in the name of tribal tradition.

Other nations, such as the so-called Utes, had played the game with mixed results, with rewards and punishments meted out justly or unjustly by political hacks, do-gooders who didn't know shit, and on rare occasions red or white statesmen who could only do what they could with the cards they'd been dealt by fickle fate.

Thanks to an old and ailing Chief Ouray and Little Big Eyes, or Interior Secretary Schurz, the two Ho Hada bands described as Mountain and South Utes were likely to hang on to their southwest corner of Colorado, subject to continued sensible behavior, as the white man defined sensible. Old Ouray had confided to whites he trusted that he'd felt like a deer signing a peace with the hunters, but *any* peace had hiding out in Canada with his Sioux enemies beat.

There were six or eight settlements spread out across the South Ute reserve, and they stopped around ten at the one consisting of a riverside trading post and wayside inn run by a Dutch family under license from the B.I.A. There were no laws against making money on an Indian reservation as long as nobody pushed whores or hard liquor.

Longarm bedded down alone without trying to find out where or with whom Wilma Thalmann or Fiona Manson might be sleeping.

In the morning, after a hearty breakfast of trade grub, Miss Wilma only sharing her maple syrup and such with her husband and their new pal, Pecos Moran, they got off to an early start with the morning crisp and dry as they followed the trace across higher ground to let the Animas wind alone through a tanglewood walled in by the bluffs of a narrow stretch. And so it went, as they followed no more than the general course of the Animas south-southwest, across the Colorado line into New Mexico Territory where the wide open spaces were open to the Homestead Act, had anyone been dumb enough to try farming that far downstream. Tosawi said old-timers he described as *Hohokum* had once grown the four sisters, Beans, Corn, Squash and Tobacco along the flood plains of the Animas. He said nobody knew much about 'em or where they'd gone. Longarm said he didn't know, either, and that the Navaho called them *Anasazi*. The only ones who knew all about 'em were professors back East who'd never met up with 'em, either.

Longarm had to back their disgusted Indian trail boss when young Lieutenant Grover and little Fiona wanted to explore some rundown cliff dwellings they spied on the far side of the river plain. He explained that even had they had the time to spare, none of the Indians passing by of late thought it polite, or wise, to disturb the spirits of long-dead strangers. He didn't tell them of the pots and such he'd seen himself over to the west on an earlier visit. He knew he'd never stop them, or the greedy Wilma, if they thought there was anything worth having over yonder.

So they rode on all day aboard their fresh ponies and then Tosawi called a halt on high ground before sundown could arouse his little brothers, the diamondbacks, and make it dangerous to move about in tricky light, uninvited by the snakes who lived in the high chaparral all around.

Longarm explained, because Tosawi chose not to, that rattlers were most dangerous when surprised; they seldom *approached* the hustle and bustle of a set-up camp. He explained, "They hide from the sun all day and hunt from sundown when the ground's still warm to say nine or ten

105

when it gets too cold for the cold-blooded critters, and they have to den up some more."

Fiona asked why they hadn't been bitten by diamondbacks the night before, riding through the sunset and beyond. He caught Tosawi's nod of approval when he explained, "We were in a hurry and our ponies were the ones risking snake bites. Ponies and other hoofed critters ain't as likely to surprise a dozing diamondback as a human pussyfooting through the stickerbrush and, be that as it may, last night was then and tonight is now, and we're deeper into semidesert at this campsite."

So nobody else argued and the poker-faced but willing Indians soon had night fires going and a row of pup tents set up, with the remuda tethered amid cottonwood brouse closer to the river. Longarm was glad none of the dudes asked why they were risking horseflesh to the storm spirit, *Yaponcha*. City folk just didn't seem to understand you had to play the odds with livestock, chancing such lives against the certainty grazing critters would decline on marginal range unless they got a crack at all the fodder and water handy.

Folk whose stock got swept away by *Yaponcha* could still walk on to safety as long as they bedded down where the waters never rose.

Sergeant Wynn rustled up some coffee, beans and bisquits to go around. Wilma Thalmann elected to dine on fancier grub and et cold in her command tent. As Wynn was rustling, Tosawi announced he'd have his young men rotate upstream as night pickets if the *taibo* would keep an eye on the trail coming up from the south.

Fiona asked if they had to worry about wild Indians. The old Ho smiled. It was hard not to smile at Fiona, and said, "Those were the good old days. At night, when the air is still, one can sometimes hear flash flooding from far away, in time to move the ponies to higher ground."

Doc Gross asked what they had to worry about from

downstream. Tosawi pointed into the darkness with his chin to say, "Strangers. Hear me, many strangers, many, ride north and south along this slope of the Shining Mountains. Those bound for Durango leave the main outlaw trails to follow *this* trail up the Animas to the silver camps and railroad tracks around Durango."

Lieutenant Grover brightened and asked if Tosawi could show him that outlaw trail on his survey charts.

Tosawi shook his head and said, "There is no *one* outlaw trail from Old Mexico to Canada through the Great Basin. There are many, too many to count if your maps showed the land the way it was. Your own outlaws know, as our raiders knew in our shining times, that a rider who follows the same trail many times is asking to be ambushed. But the canyon lands and basin-and-range country further west offer many ways to ride. Many. With only a few . . . how do you say, bottlenecks widely spaced across mostly wide open range. This river valley we are riding down is one such bottleneck. More than one trail from the south leads more than one sort of rider on up to Durango. I don't think anyone following one of the outlaw trails tonight would want to attack any party this size. But as one should not step on our little brothers with rattles after dark, one should keep the night fires going and post guards so that no strangers may stumble over us in the dark and get silly!"

Longarm said he'd take the first watch after bedtime and asked who wanted to relieve him say two hours later. Pecos Moran of the Texas Rangers allowed he had nothing better to do. Longarm didn't ask why. Sneaking into a tent with Miss Wilma would be risky as hell.

Lieutenant Grover volunteered himself and Sergeant Wynn for the wee small hours. So Doc Frank sighed, "Nu, I couldn't volunteer for the early shift? All right, you can wake me up before dawn and that should do it?"

Agent Thalmann hadn't volunteered, and they told Sister Fiona not to be silly when she asked when it might be her turn. She looked hurt. So Longarm explained, "The Doc will barely have time to take over before it'll be time to saddle up and ride on, Sis."

She said, "Pooh, you boys never let us have any fun!"

Everyone there but Thalman and Tosawi laughed. The four younger Indians wouldn't have got it, but they were at their own fire fifty feet away.

After enjoying a modest but protracted meal, they jawed a spell about the trail ahead before Thalmann and then the doc allowed they'd turn in. So Longarm rose to fetch his Winchester from his pup tent and mosey out into the chaparral to the south.

Night picket hadn't bothered him as much as kitchen police in his army days, albeit he felt both pleasures should be enjoyed in moderation. The sky above was putting on a swell display above him, with the Milky Way you seldom saw in towns with streetlamps running catty-corner as a ghostly glow against star-spangled black velvet and more falling stars than a really greedy kid could wish on a clear August night.

The first time he moved in to throw more deadwood on the night fire he saw everyone else had turned in. Strolling back to the south, he idly wondered who'd be in old Wilma's tent and sort of hoped nobody but Fiona would be in hers.

He told himself not to study on the awfully pretty but not-too-bright little thing as he paced back and forth under the falling stars. For even the gals smart enough to follow his drift tended to get all wet-eyed when he explained how a tumbleweed cuss wearing a badge for a living had no call making promises, the lucky cuss.

His two hours on picket passed surprisingly fast, and when he went to the tent next to his own to wake Moran, the Texan cussed him and allowed he'd just been getting to first base with that Jersey Lily the Prince of Wales seemed so fond of.

But old Pecos got up to rub the sleep gum from his eyes, have a look at the night fire, and thank Longarm for that fresh load of brightly but quickly burning deadwood before he ambled off into the dark with his own saddle gun.

The Indian trail hands had naturally gathered dead willow and cottonwood from down along the Animas, rimrock sage burning even faster and piñon or cedar off higher ridges not being handy.

Longarm put his Winchester to bed but stood outside to light a last smoke, still having a heap on his mind and knowing how easy it was to set a pup tent afire by smoking inside the same.

As he shook out the match stem and broke it to make sure it was out, a familiar she-male voice trilled, "Can't you sleep, either, Buck?"

He moved toward Fiona's barely visible form to softly warn her to keep it down lest they wake others doing their best on the hard ground.

As the two of them drifted farther from the firelight by tacit consent, the chestnut-headed gal said she was sleepy enough after all that riding down from the trading post, but too worried about those *snakes* to lie still under bedding spread across the *ground*!

She asked if it was true you could keep rattlesnakes at bay with a hemp rope looped around your bedroll in the dust. He laughed and told her, "Not hardly. A snake would be proud to slither over a throw-rope if it cared to. But since it seldom cares to, a heap of folk who've spent the night inside such a magic loop now swear by it. I reckon a heap of religious notions got started that way. You don't step on a crack and, sure enough, when you get home your mother's back hasn't been busted. But like I told you before, snakes slow down as the earth cools off after sundown, and the Indians who live out this way with 'em consider them pals. The Pueblos in particular value them as rat catchers and encourage 'em to hunt in their cornfields."

"Don't they ever get bitten by rattlesnakes?" she asked.

He said, "Not as often as you might expect. Snakes can't eat anything they can't swallow whole. So they've no call to strike at anything bigger than a rabbit, and it takes a big diamondback to put away a rabbit. Bigger critters bit by snakes are the victims of misunderstandings. You'd stab an elephant if you thought it was fixing to step on you. But would you try to swallow it, or go looking for an elephant to stab?"

She giggled at the picture and said, "Well, if you think it safe, now, I am awfully tired."

So he started to walk her back to her own pup tent, playing by ear what might or might not happen once they got there.

But before they got there all hell broke loose!

First came the cry of a familiar voice calling out, "Halt! Who goes there?" followed by a fusillade of gunshots from at least two guns, a .38 and a .45 if Longarm was any judge, and then Pecos Moran cried out, "Hot damn in San Antone! I think I *got* him!"

But he hadn't, it developed, once everyone was up and scouting out in all directions by torchlight. One of the Indians found an empty Harrington and Richardson whore pistol, or "Detective Special," as the sneaky little pisso-liver was marketed. But that was all, and whether a Texan on picket had winged him or not, the sneak had vanished into the darkness from which he'd come.

A good spell later, as things were starting to settle some, it was Pecos Moran who called Longarm over by their neighboring tents to observe, "I know why I'm still alive, pard. Where were *you* when the rascal shot the shit out of both our tents?"

Longarm stepped closer to hold his own cottonwood torch closer as he morosely regarded bullet holes, a lot of bullet holes, through the tan canvas low enough to play hell with anyone sleeping inside.

The man with a ranger badge gleaming in the torchlight from the front of his shirt said, "I know why they were after *me*. How come they were after *you*? Are you sure you've been leveling with me, old son? Who might you be for real, a bounty hunter, or another lawman on your way to investigate that same haunted whorehouse in Animas Point?"

Chapter 13

Since he had to say something, Longarm allowed he was still Buck Crawford, a federal paper pusher assigned to the B.I.A. as a guide, but had to admit he'd been reading wanted fliers as he filed 'em and meant to look that mysterious whorehouse over, if they didn't shoot him before he could get there.

Moran said, "There you go. I knew there had to be some reason for that so-called reporter in Durango to ask about you. They already knew who *I* was. They're on the prod for visiting lawmen and . . ."

"How come?" Longarm cut in, "Seeing none of the lawmen who've gone before us have managed to catch any haunts in the act? Why should we be any different to them?"

The Texan modestly replied, "I don't know about you, but it just so happens I'm sort of famous for tracking down wants they send me out to bring in. Anyone can see someone down yonder has been flim-flamming lesser lawmen with some trick they're afraid a *slicker* lawman might be able to see through. So that accounts for them shooting up *my* tent just now. Your turn."

Longarm said, "We might be seeing tigers in the wallpaper. They might not have had a particular target in mind. If they were yonder in the dark any time at all they should have seen it was *you* out on picket. So why didn't they just get you betwixt them and the night fire and blow you off your feet instead of pegging away at your empty tent, Pecos?"

Longarm wanted to kick himself for the slip when the Texan said, "By Jimmies, that's right! They couldn't have been after me! They were after *you!* From out in the chaparral they'd have seen you waking me up and sending me out like a lamb to slaughter. But if they were scouting from a distance, they might not have been too clear about which tent was yours. So they shot up both of them to make sure!"

Longarm shook his head to say, "That don't work, neither. If they were watching all the time, they'd have seen I never ducked into either tent. Fortunate for the both of us, I was off a ways . . . taking a leak, when . . . What happened?"

Moran said, "I spotted movement, off to the west, and asked some stars winking on and off near the horizon who they were. When my polite question was replied to with pistol shots, I replied in kind, to empty the wheel of my side arm at the muzzle flashes. I heard that thud you hear when lead smacks into meat and the clink of that .38 landing in the grit. The rest you know. I think I winged at least one of 'em, and now I'm kicking myself because I drew and fired my six-gun without even thinking about the carbine in my left hand! I'd have dropped the cocksucker for certain had I emptied by *carbine* at them muzzle flashes."

Then he added, "I see your point. The rascal couldn't have been watching too close when he moved in to smoke up the camp. What was that about tigers in the wallpaper?"

Longarm explained, "Our eyes are trained to see pat-

114

terns, whether they're there or not. That Eye-talian as-
tronomer discovered canals on the planet Mars, whether
they're real or not, because them dim blotches *ought* to
be connected up some way. Little kids scare themselves
with scary faces and kid-eating tigers staring out at them
from wallpaper designs the artist who designed 'em never
intended. When we ain't too sure what we're looking at,
we make up patterns that ain't there."

Moran nodded thoughtfully and said, "You mean like
dead whores and owlhoot riders haunting a dinky trail
town in the middle of nowhere!"

That had been a statement rather than a question. But
Longarm still answered, "That's about the size of it."

So after some fitful sleep and an early start, they all
rode into Animas Point the next afternoon and nobody
argued when the imperious Wilma Thalmann decreed that
was far enough for the day as she, for one, meant to spend
a civilized night in the one hotel in town.

The Animas ran past the trail town through a bottleneck
betwixt high bluffs, with the town looking down on the
floodplain from its aptly named point of high ground. After that, there was one main street running east and west
from the overlook into the sage and chaparral of marginal
range. There was a municipal corral, but old Tosawi said
they'd be swapping the ponies from his reservation for
Spanish saddle mules, not bothering to explain the country
ahead would be even harder on horseflesh, or that there'd
be no place to find fresh mounts before they made it all
the way down to Fort Defiance.

Leaving their Indians to work that out, the B.I.A. party
and the tagalong Texan checked into the hotel with their
personal possibles. They inhaled an early restaurant supper together, next door, before they split up to explore the
town by the remaining daylight.

There wasn't much of Animas Point to explore. It
seemed a trail-stop shopping center cum general post of-

fice for such cattle spreads as there were within a day's ride. Lieutenant Grover said he didn't see how one drove cattle to market from such out-of-the-way range. Longarm let the Texan tell the army man how cattle spreads west of the Great Divide served beef to mining camps, military outposts and Indian agencies. Longarm could only nod when Moran explained how the notorious Lincoln County War, west of the Pecos he was named for, had been over who got to sell beef to the Mescalero reservation and the colored cav at Fort Stanton.

Longarm agreed they were still an easy cattle drive from the Ute reserves and Durango beyond. It was his turn to look smart when he explained the B.I.A. preferred to feed Indians beef on the hoof than have them riding off the reservation on so-called hunting expeditions. He added, "Everyone but the late Agent Meeker seemed to know the North Utes raised ponies for riding and shot meat on sight. Some Caddo and Cherokee have taken up cowboy habits of late. But most Indians still prefer to play Indian when it comes to bringing home the bacon."

Longarm, the Texan and the two army engineers continued the conversation in the surprisingly handsome saloon across the way from that livery where Tosawi was working out their next day's riding and packing.

Sergeant Wynn was sure there'd be action behind the doors facing out onto the second-story wrap-around mezzanine and drifted down the bar to make friends with the regulars. Longarm and the others were talking about Spanish saddle mules in dry country when the sergeant got back to them, reporting with a sly grin, "They tell me there ain't no action here in the center of town no more. Prissy town law and a ladies' temperance chapter put all the cribs upstairs out of business. But they tell me there's this whorehouse off to the west, just outside the city limits, where a man can bed two gals at once for the price of one in bigger towns, save on payday nights!"

As Longarm and Moran exchanged thoughtful looks, the second john said, "Just our luck Tosawi's holding our horses! I don't know about you gents, but I'm a long way from home and to tell the truth I've commenced to have impure thoughts about even Miss Wilma, trying not to think of her and Sister Fiona undressed and in bed to either side of me for many a night this side of Chicago. Old Sarge and me did get laid on State Street, and things were wild as we'd heard!"

Sergeant Wynn suggested, "Begging the lieutenant's pardon, it ain't too far to walk. Less than seven furlongs, or so they tell me."

Pecos Moran asked, "What are we waiting for, then? Old Wilma is taken and little Fiona looks to be cherry. So let's get going and last one in is a sissy!"

Longarm knew he'd never get a better chance to visit the place with his own badge out of sight. So the four of them finished their beers and lit out to get laid as they strode west into the sunset at the far end of Main Street. Seven furlongs was well short of a mile.

Such street as there was gave way to wagon ruts across dusty grit before they could approach the three-story, mansard-roofed barn-red frame structure, springing from otherwise open range sort of freakish, like a leftover circus prop left behind by careless clowns. As the four of them trudged closer, the front door opened and a fat lady wearing a red velvet and whaleboned bustier with her bare tits out over the top stepped out on the veranda to howdy them and say they were just in time for the quitting-time special.

She wasn't wearing anything but pubic hair below the bustier and didn't have to explain she meant they offered a special for men dropping by on their way home after their *own* quitting time.

Taking the lead, Longarm replied in a worldly voice that they'd like a drink and a look at the merchandise

117

before they decided how long they might want to stay. The madam or head whore, it was hard to tell, led the way inside, where an even less modestly dressed lady with hair that just didn't match, above and below, lounged against the bar and directed another naked gal behind the same to serve their visitors their famous Taos Lighting Sunsets.

As the four of them bellied up to the bar, Longarm quietly asked Moran, "See anybody you know?"

"We seem to be the only customers at this hour," the Texan replied, adding, "None of these drabs look famous. But I was told the one and original Lola Montez performed her notorious spider dance out this way on occasion, stark-ass naked save for them rubber spiders."

The red- and black-haired naked lady lounging on Moran's far side had overheard, it seemed, when she calmly remarked, "Lola Montez died years ago in Brooklyn, New York State, middle-aged and feeling poorly, cowboy. But I'll let you peel spiders off my hide if that's your pleasure and you know where to find some."

Longarm wasn't surprised when Moran calmly asked her if she took it brown, and she replied with a gallant shrug, "Dosen't everybody?"

By this time another whore had materialized on Longarm's other side to ask if he'd treat her to a drinky-poo. He saw the two army men had other whores flirting with them. Not a one in the remuda inspired a man who'd laid some right pretty women in his day.

He told Moran, "I've seen enough. Anyone else you were fixing to meet here knew you were coming, and this trade liquor tastes like somebody's already drunk it. I'm heading back to the hotel. It ain't for me to say when or if the rest of you might be leaving."

The whore who'd been begging him for a drinky-poo asked him if he was queer for boys. Longarm ignored her. Pecos Moran shrugged and said, "Hate to think I'd walked all this way for nothing. You go on back to the hotel, and we'll join you later, Longarm."

They both caught the slip at the same time and slapped leather as one. Moran's .45-caliber Peacemaker cleared its holster a split second sooner. Longarm's .44 Frontier, made by the same firm to fire double-action, roared a split second ahead of Moran's single-action.

A split second was all it took when the result was two hundred grains of hot lead smashing through the breast-bone and into the heart. Moran fired his one and only round into the floorboards betweeen them.

He tried to hold himself upright with his left hand gripping the bar as he died enough to let go his smoking six-gun and collapse at Longarm's feet.

Lieutenant Grover came unstuck to gasp, "Jesus H. Christ, Buck! What was *that* all about?"

The naked whore who'd been trying to cadge a glass of water at the going rates for tequila sobbed, "I seen it all! The loser should have been the winner 'cause he drew first! But this big moose moves like spit on a hot stove!"

"Yeah, but *why*?" insisted the army engineer.

Longarm said, "Ain't sure. I caught him in a slip of the tongue. He knew I'd caught him in a slip of the tongue. I have reason to suspect that was him and nobody else but him who smoked up my tent last night under the impression I was in it. He'd brought that cheap .38 along with him as a ruse. He let out that loud challenge to nobody at all and emptied both six-guns into his tent and mine, knowing for certain his own tent was unoccupied and doubtless favoring mine with all his army .45-28 rounds. Then he lobbed the empty Harrington and Richardson farther out for that Indian kid to find as he two-faced up to me in hopes of another chance farther along. How do you like it so far?"

Grover said, "Well, I know for a fact he was two-faced. He's been fucking Miss Wima behind her husband's back.

But why did he have it in for you? They told us you were a file clerk at the federal office building in Denver. If that's true, why would the Texas Rangers be after you, and why wouldn't he simply arrest you if he *did* have a warrant on you?"

The whore who said she'd seen it all said, "I know! He's a famous gunslick and that poor dead ranger was afraid to arrest him. You had to be there. And no—I'm going upstairs to put some duds on before the *law* gets here. Coming, ladies?"

The three male survivors had the parlor floor to themselves and the late Pecos Moran when, sure enough, an older gent and three others, all sporting mail-order stars of polished pewter, tore in, guns drawn, to demand some damned explanations for all them gunshots just now.

Fortunately, Longarm had reloaded and put his .44-40 back in its cross-draw holster by then. So as the town law covered the three of them less certainly, Longarm quietly said, "I'd be Buck Crawford and I cannot tell a lie. Me and these two army men are with a B.I.A. team headed for Fort Defiance. You can check with our leader, Agent Martin Luther Thalmann at the hotel in town. This gent on the floor joined us in Durango. Said he was a Texas Ranger named James or Pecos Moran. I've reason to doubt that could be true. I've no idea where the real Pecos Moran might be this evening, but this phoney one just drew on me for reasons I'm still trying to fathom."

A she-male voice from the stairs trilled, "He's telling it true, Stubby. I seen it all. The one in black denim drew first. Before that, they were talking friendly. That nice looking one who won gave him no sensible cause to draw. He just said he was headed back to town and the next thing I knew they were shooting it out."

The town law called Stubby bent over the cadaver to suddenly gasp, "Son of a bitch if this one wasn't a Texas Ranger!"

As he straightened up with his drawn gun trained thoughtfully on Longarm, the undercover federal lawman suggested, "Do you wire Austin, I'll bet you dollars to doughnuts they'll say he wasn't ever one of their own and had no jurisdiction out here in New Mexico Territory in any case."

Old Stubby said, "That well may be. It makes more sense than a Texas lawman slapping leather on the B.I.A. but I hope we all understand not a one of you gents will be leaving town before I get me a handle on just what happened out here this evening?"

Chapter 14

The forced layover offered Longarm the chance to snoop around Animas Point a spell longer without tipping his mitt. But both the Thalmann's were sore as hell at him for shooting the cuss old Wilma had been fooling with on the side. Agent Thalmann was just in a hurry to get it on down the road and set up his own Chindi Agency, Longarm felt sure.

Longarm and the two army men signed depositions for the county coroner when they got back to town. Longarm didn't ask whether Grover and Wynn would be going back out to that whorehouse after things at the hotel settled down. He headed for the telegraph office, himself.

Since it paid to ask dumb questions, once Longarm had composed a coded progress report for his aunt in Denver he casually asked the Western Union clerk how come he'd seen no telegraph wires coming down from Durango.

The telegrapher explained they had no need of the same, thanks to the speed of dots and dashes along an electric wire. He said, "They just started building, up Durango way. We've been here a spell. Our wire runs south to Fort Defiance, then east to Santa Fe, from whence branch wires lead in all directions. If you wired someboy in Durango the message would go by way of Santa Fe, then up to Pueblo and out this way some more to Durango. Ain't modern science wonderful?"

Longarm decided that made more sense than a web of wire running from every town to every other town, and he knew it was true you could send a cable from Denver to London town, now, faster than you could Denver to, say, Fort Collins or even Golden in the nearby Front Range by rail. He idly wondered if someday they'd have those new Bell telephones hooked up the same way. It seemed sort of spooky when you considered it might someday be possible to talk dirty to a gal it could take a month to get next to if she took you up on it!

Still on edge, Longarm went back to that big saloon across from the nearby livery for a nightcap and any action worth reporting to his aunt in Denver.

The place was nigh empty, save for some locals playing penny-ante stud at a corner table. The barkeep agreed things were usually quiet that far from payday. It would have been cruel to ask how they ever stayed in business. Longarm could see the place had been built to handle bigger crowds in wilder times. Things were ever booming or busting in the Four Corners country, what with military campaigns and gold rushes busting out only to fizzle away with nothing much to show for all the effort but dramatic scenery only the native flora and fauna had much use for. Things around Animas Point might or might not be picking up now that the more serious destination of Durango lay at the north end of the military trace and postal route from Fort Defiance. But things sure seemed quiet that night.

He went back to the hotel and mounted the stairs to his room. He was fixing to put the hired key in the lock when he spied a match stem on the hall runner, just under the lower hinge he'd wedged it under when he'd locked away his borrowed saddle and other shit.

A big gray cat got up to stretch and swish its fuzzy tail in Longarm's guts as he muttered, "Right, that other one, who said he was a reporter, up Durango way!"

So he came close to shooting little Sister Fiona when he burst in to throw down on her with his six-gun and a snarl of, "Freeze, you motherfucker!"

Fiona gasped, "Is that any way to talk to a lady, Buck?"

To which he could only reply, "I thought you were somebody else. Forget what I just said about your poor mother, but you just scared the liver and lights out of me!"

She giggled and said, "That made two of us! I let myself in to wait for you when I discovered my room key fits all the locks on this floor. I wanted to tell you what I've figured out about that mean Texas Ranger who tried to shoot you, earlier."

As he calmed some in the tricky light from outside, the oil lamp by the bed being naturally trimmed during his absence, Longarm saw she was wearing a chocolate bathrobe that went well with the long chestnut waves she'd unpinned for the night. He shut the hall door. That shed even less light on the subject. But had she wanted him to light the lamp, she could have said so.

He asked her what she'd figured out. Fiona said, "I don't think he was really a Texas Ranger. I think he must have been a crook, and I'll bet that was *him* shooting up your tent last night, and aren't you glad you were with me instead of alone in bed at the time?"

Longarm chuckled wistfully and remarked he found it sort of tedious to be alone in bed at anytime. She moved closer in the dim light as she languidly replied she'd noticed that. So he took her in his arms, as most men would have, but felt obliged to warn her, "I'm only going as far as that uncharted canyon with you-all. I won't be staying whether we find any lost tribe of Indians or not, so . . ."

"For heaven's sake!" she cut in, coming barely to his chest as she threw her arms around him, "Did you think

I was out to marry up and settle down, Buck? I'm only out to get laid, you big goof!"

So he kissed her as she let her robe fall open to thrust her bare pubic mound against his fly as she tongued him deep, and that felt way better than being in bed alone as well. But when they came up for air, he still felt honor bound to ask if she'd reached the age of consent, no offense.

She laughed and said, "I'm twenty-seven, and it serves you right for taking me for a teenager. I've tried to grow a beard but I just can't manage. Is that what's been making you treat me like a little girl, you big silly? Even if I was a kid, I'm a trained nurse. So you couldn't get me in trouble if you tried!"

He said, "Well, you can't blame a man for trying!" and they were both laughing as they fell across the bed together and he entered her without even taking off his hat.

That made for a swell surprise for the both of them as they found what a tight match his old organ grinder was to her ring-dang-doo. But he had to agree she had a point when she allowed she'd never fornicated with a man wearing a Stetson and six-gun before. So he rolled off just long enough to toss everything to the winds and start fresh with her robe out of the way as well.

Unlike the more willowy and more tender Marsha Olan of fond memory, the smaller but more curvaceous Fiona went at her fucking as seriously as that dusky Cecilia back in Denver, albeit Fiona's button nose parted his pubic hair entirely different when she went down on him to get it up some more. Mentally comparing the totally different ways the two equally wild young things fucked and sucked inspired a heroic erection with which to pursue the matter further, and Fiona said she loved it when he hit bottom, hard, with her small shapely legs spread wide as legs could go without ripping off.

Neither knew, nor would they have really cared, that at

126

the moment they were coming together for the third time Lieutenant Grover was responding to a gentle but persistent tapping on his own door.

When he opened it to see Wilma Thalmann there in a black silk kimono, the young army engineer sincerely regretted the two dollars he'd just spent at that whorehouse on the outskirts of town. For he suspected he knew what she was really after when Wilma ducked inside to whisper, "We have to talk! That little snip, Sister Fiona, is having an affair with Buck Crawford, right down the hall!"

Grover laughed and said, "You don't say! Well, it couldn't happen to a better sport, and what do you expect *me* to do about it, ask for sloppy seconds?"

Wilma threw the inside bolt on the door as she demanded, "Is that any way to speak to a lady, ah, Harry? The man's a killer, and she's so young and innocent!"

Taking her in his arms, the young but far from innocent army man replied, "I'd never talk that way to a *lady* and Buck's not a killer. I was there when he shot that other man you've been fucking in self-defense!"

"Oh, my God, how can you *say* such things!" she sobbed, even as she failed to resist his firm grasp on her bare derriere, underneath her kimono. So he told her it was easy, and she didn't resist when he moved her over to the bed and lowered her to the mattress.

But thanks to that three-ways-for-two-dollars session on the outskirts of town, he'd have never managed to get it up if the very shapely and now stark-naked brunette hadn't known how to help a bashful lover out, and damned if she didn't suck better than that professional he'd *paid* for a French lesson out at that big red whorehouse.

Hence, once she had him hard and assumed a coy position on her hands and knees, the soldier knew just where she wanted him to shove it, albeit, as he did so she gyrated her generous rump to gasp, "Oh, no! you have it in the wrong hole! Not even my *husband* does it *that* way!"

Grover calmly replied he'd been wondering why she fucked around on the side as he grasped a hip bone in either hand to Greek her hot and heavy with his bare feet on the braided rug beside the bed.

She told him he was a vile beast and a fresh kid besides as she arched her spine to take him deeper into her bowels, dilating and contracting her rectum with the practiced skill of a dedicated daughter of Sodom. She didn't mind at all when it took him so much longer than most men to come in her that way. She held out as long as she could before she reached down to strum her own banjo in time with his thrusts, sobbing, "Don't laugh at me, Harry! I'm always so certain I'll be able to climax . . . naturally, with a dick up my ass. But it seems to carry me right to the very edge and just leaves me hanging there unless I . . . Oh, Jesus H. Christ I'm coming, and God bless that Buck Crawford for shooting that Texan who didn't know how to treat me so fine!"

So a good time was had by all but her husband and Doc Frank down the hall. Tosawi and the other Indians had friends in Animas Point.

The next morning, seeing they were stuck in town until the local coroner released them, Longarm and Fiona went sight-seeing, afoot with their duds on. She wanted to walk the kinks out of her legs and he needed the excuse to poke about without seeming nosey. Folk who gave the fish-eye to a stranger strolling by never seemed to worry about a couple doing the very same thing.

Fiona wanted to window-shop, and he encouraged her vice. It gave him time to gaze all about from one spot before moving on to repeat the process farther along. Fiona said the prices posted in the window of a dress shop were scandalous. When she said she could have bought the same summer frock for less in Washington D.C.,

Longarm told her prices had ever been higher out that way, explaining, "Mine owners and cattle barons can afford the freight charges. *Poor* folk out this way or any other ways can't afford such fancy frocks at any price."

She didn't sound convinced as they drifted on.

They met up with Doc Frank in front of a boarded-up opera house, if the sign above the once ornate entrance was to be believed. As they joined the doc, Frank asked, "Can you believe it? An *opera house* in such a location?"

Longarm pointed to a sun-faded three-sheet announcing the showing of Verdi's Rigoletto to say, "Must have been built back in the '60s when there was more going on out this way. I think Mr. Verdi writ that one before the war betwixt the states and, *during* that war, all ned was going on out this way, what with Confederate raiders, Indian raiders, flash-in-the-pan gold rushes and all."

The Baltimore physician grimaced and said, "Just the same, as my uncle Morris the Realtor used to say, there are three things you have to make sure of before you start any business. Location, location and *location*! Nu, you'd build an opera house in *this* location?"

Longarm said, "I wouldn't build an opera house anywheres, and you can see that whoever built this one, here, soon learned your uncle Morris the Realtor had a point. They shut down and walked away with no buyers for the property. There's other boarded-over shops and one saloon that's failed here in Animas Point."

He let that sink in and added, "You have to pick a *really* poor location to fail in the saloon business. There just ain't enough travel along this military trail to justify a town this size at this location."

Nobody argued, and they drifted back together for noon dinner near the hotel, where they were joined by the town law, old Stubby Croft as it turned out.

Joining them for coffee, the old-timer told Longarm, "Lucky for you, Mr. Crawford, Austin confirms your suspicion you never shot their Corporal Moran of the Texas Rangers at all. He's on duty, alive and well in La Mesa, Texas, even as we speak."

He sipped some coffee and slyly asked, "Would you care to know who you really shot, yesterday evening?"

When Longarm said he'd sure been feeling curious about that, old Stubby said, "We just identified him from a tattoo described on his wanted flyer. His real name was Jed Farnsworth. He was a hired gun. Had the real Pecos Moran met up with him in Texas, where they both hailed from, the ranger would have shot him just as *you* did. He was wanted bad. More places than one for a whole string of killings!"

Longarm smiled thinly as he replied, "Do tell? There should have been some bounty money posted on such a rascal, no?"

The old-timer shoved away from the table suggesting, "Why don't you let *us* worry about such picky details? Coroner just told me to tell you-all you're free to ride on, seeing the investigation has ended as of now."

After he'd risen and left, Doc Frank looked puzzled and demanded, "That's it? They don't want to hold even a coroner's hearing?"

Before Longarm could explain, the innocent-looking Fiona shook her chestnut curls to declare, "Honestly, Doctor, you never seem to surprise us with your grasp on worldly matters! Do you really need me to draw a diagram on the blackboard?"

Frank looked sincerely puzzled, brightened, and said, "Oh, they don't want to share any reward money with outsiders, right?"

To which Longarm could only reply, "That's about the size of it, Doc. But didn't Agent Thalmann say he was in a hurry to move on?"

Chapter 15

Lest the local authorities change their minds, the B.I.A. party rode out that afternoon, sitting taller in their saddles. Spanish saddle mules were about the size of thoroughbred horses, sharing the same Arab ancestry on their maternal sides. You got a sensible mule by breeding a mare with a jackass. When you subjected a jenny to the advances of a stallion you wound up with a pathetic hinny instead of a mule, if she lived.

Fiona hadn't known the difference betwixt a mule and a burro or donkey until he explained it to her later that night, in a pup tent. She said it made her feel horny to think of a little donkey and a big horse in unnatural union. She said a schoolmate had once had a pet rabbit that fucked cats, but nothing happened when critters were so different. She said that when she'd studied biology, she'd found out it wasn't true that humans mating with critters produced such monsters as satyrs and mermaids, so burning people at the stake for such fun back in the Middle Ages had been wicked superstition.

He agreed death by fire seemed sort of severe punishment for taking animal loving to extremes, but heaps of laws that seemed needlessly strict made sense and vice versa, there being heaps of things that weren't against the law that would have been, had *he* had anything to say about it. He felt no call to add he'd have left those unregistered Indians who didn't seem to be bothering anybody in peace. Then he did her dog style to let her study on what it might feel like to rut with a critter.

She said it made her feel dirty. She didn't ask him to stop.

Next morning before sunup they were on their way south of the east-west San Juan canyon complex the Animas and heaps of others drained into. A couple of trail breaks on, Longarm had just noticed there were no telegraph poles in sight when Lieutenant Grover reined in beside him to ask, "Buck, could you say why we don't seem to be following that military route to Fort Defiance?"

Longarm replied, "Not hardly, but I mean to find out."

The shavetail tagged along as Longarm heeled his mule up the column to overtake old Tosawi and politely ask the old Indian what the fuck he thought he was up to.

Tosawi replied with a puzzled frown, "Didn't you people want me to lead you to Fort Defiance?"

Grover was the one who pointed out they didn't seem to be following the mapped out route to Fort Defiance.

Tosawi snorted, "Of course not. Do you think I am crazy? Why would I lead a party this size along that trail laid out for army columns and freight wagons to follow?"

Longarm nodded and told the army man, "I follow his drift. He knows what he's doing. We're traveling lighter, using way less fodder, fuel and water. We can afford to take shortcuts that would be too risky for outfits apt to suck water holes dry, with thirsty stock left over. He's following one of them unmapped trails better known to wild game, Indians or mayhaps outlaws."

Tosawi grunted, "I thought you had to be . . . who I thought you had to be. You are not stupid enough to be anybody else riding for the B.I.A. This is only one of the ways we used to ride through enemy hunting grounds in the good old days before you *taibos* crushed our favorite enemies and turned them into sheepherders and silversmiths. In our shining times, all you see around you was Navaho country. Blue sleeves with mountain howitzers were safe enough on their own wagon trace to Fort Defiance. Before the Navaho were tamed by Rope Thrower they could be dangerous. Even *we* had to be careful in Navaho country.

"We followed trails made by our brothers, the big horns, the deer and of course, Old Man Coyote. Some stretches of the way ahead were laid out by the Hohokum who lived around here too long ago to remember. I will show you places where Hohokum still wait for something, all dried up but smiling, smiling, in their stone houses on the sides of cliffs. We Ho fear nothing. So when we found out the Navaho were afraid of dead Hohokum, we followed trails they never used through canyons where many Hohokum still sit, smiling, in their feather robes. The Navaho were good fighters. They made fine enemies. But they were stupid, stupid, about stars and dead people!"

As they rode on, Longarm explained to the army man how Dine-speaking Navaho and their Apache cousins had learned to raid on overcast moonless nights because they suspected stars might be looking down at them. He asked Tosawi if his own nation had ever tried to spook their favorite enemies by pretending to be *chindi*. The old Ute Scout made a wry face and replied, "Sometimes. It didn't always work. Navaho shoot ghosts or people they take for ghosts on sight."

Young Grover asked if the Navaho thought it was possible to kill a ghost, or *chindi*, as they put it.

Tosawi said, "Of course not. That is how they tell if someone they meet on the trail at dusk is a ghost or a real person. When they shoot it, and they see it fall down, they know they have only killed a real person. If they shoot it and it does not fall down, they know it is a ghost. So they run away as fast as they can. That is how you tell a Navaho or Apache from other people. If you meet a stranger near dusk, and he shoots at you without asking who you are, you know he is a Navaho or Apache."

Longarm explained, "Not the ones we call Navaho, lately. The two designations started out as one. Same lingo, same notions. Same ways at first. Then the ones we call Navaho learned the advantages of a cornfield and a herd of sheep next to just robbing somebody every supper time. Navaho is a Pueblo word for a hoe farmer. Even before Kit Carson calmed them down, they were starting to civilize themselves by swapping coin silver jewelry and fine saddle blankets for Basque sheepherding shirts, Merino sheep and so forth. Their less progressive cousins we're still having trouble with were and are rightly described as enemies, or Apache, in the Pima Pueblo dialect."

"Those *civilized* Navaho were the ones *we* had the most trouble with!" said Tosawi, explaining, "Once they got to trading with the Mexicans they had more guns and better horses than the Apache, who fought like wicked children next to real people. Navaho ranged farther, in greater numbers. Later, you *taibo* shit on us all. But it was a good thing when Rope Thrower Carson led us into Canyon de Chelly to fight them their own way—dirty, dirty, dirty!"

Longarm explained to Grover, "Being a mountain man first and an irregular cavalryman second, Kit Carson had learned to think like the Indians he was fighting. He knew the braves would hole up amid the cliffs of Canyon de Chelly. He never tried to root 'em out of the sky. Him and his riders, red and white, rode up and down their canyon stronghold herding their weeeping woman and children ahead of them as they burned all the shelters, stored supplies and even firewood. Then they shot all the

Navaho stock, mostly sheep and a heap of ponies. They hardly killed any Indians at all."

"We didn't have to!" Tosawi gloated, "When they saw they faced a winter with nothing to eat and no blankets to cover them, they had to give up. We marched them, on foot, far to the east, across the Pecos, and the army put them to work digging ditches and planting fruit trees. They hated it. They wept like women. Some killed themselves. Then, after they had been treated like captive women for a time, Rope Thrower Carson spoke kindly for them and they were told they could go home to their canyon lands again to raise sheep and weave blankets and hammer silver and leave other people alone."

He sighed and confessed, "It spoiled them as enemies. How was anyone to know the sister-fucking Navaho would keep their word? Nobody had ever heard of a sister-fucking Navaho keeping his word! But they have, and now we have nobody to hate but their Apache kinsman, and you *taibo*, of course."

"Sister fucking?" Grover asked.

Longarm shook his head and said, "Not hardly. A paid-up Navaho won't even speak to his mother-in-law, and at dances they have to compare family trees dozens of generations back lest they wind up messing with a distant cousin. Most Indians are more horrified by incest than cannibalism. That's likely why they accuse one another of it so often. Lying is considered almost as bad by our so-called Navaho, albeit the ones we call Apache glory in lying to outsiders. Makes for tricky relationships an Indian agent or soldier blue can fuck up at his peril. For example, no offense to Tosawi, here, it's considered all right for a Navaho *woman* to lie, cheat and steal. So on a Navaho reserve's trading post, they pay no mind to the boys and men, who never shoplift, but watch the woman and girls like hawks lest they walk out with the cash till under their loose skirts!"

"Hear me, they are sister-fucking liars. I have spoken," Tosawi insisted.

Tosawi led them on, and on, to have everyone in the party but Longarm totally lost within seventy-two hours, and Longarm not dead certain where he was when he tried to point their position out to the army survey team in a blank patch on their main land office chart. The lieutenant allowed that if Longarm was right, the crazy old Indian was saving them miles as the crow might fly.

They were riding Spanish saddle mules instead, so they had to zig and zag, albeit not nigh as much as that military route meant for more serious outfits.

Tosawi led them high through forests of cedar and pine. He led them low through floodplains choked by tanglewoods of crack willow and cottonwood with poison oak and thorny yellow rose thrown in. He led them across sage flats and alkali flats where nothing grew at all and warned then not to let their mounts muzzle any rain puddles they might cross. But he mostly led them through canyons, allowing it was safer to ride *through* the pumpkin than across it.

Sometimes they had to almost ride around the circle Lieutenant Grover said they were riding in. Other times Tosawi seemed to be leading them the wrong way entire. But each night they stopped, the positions Longarm and Sergeant Wynn worked out on the chart had them ten to twenty miles closer to Fort Defiance and, better yet, Tosawi and his Indian kids never failed to rustle up enough fodder, fuel and water for a comfortable stay.

The others began to see what Longarm meant by Tosawi reminding him of Miss Goldilocks in that bedtime story. Never too much, never too little and just about right for a party their size and its stock. A wagon train or cavalry column might have found the going rougher if not impossible, for half the time they used up all the dry deadwood by morning or left a water hole little more than a mud puddle by the time they moved on.

Now and again they spotted signs left by others traveling the old Ho Hada war trail, albeit the thrown shoe in one canyon and the oat-flecked horse turds in another read white rider rather than red. Tosawi told them not to expect much Indian signs. His own kind seldom rode that far south whilst the Navaho stayed out of the canyons he kept choosing. He said that was why he kept choosing them.

When Agent Thalmann asked if those mysterious Chindi might be trying to avoid the Navaho, old Tosawi shrugged and decided, "Papago, maybe. Papago don't like it on the rimrocks where it gets cold after dark. Papago wear nothing, nothing, and, like us, have always hated Navaho. But if there are any real people at all between Fort Defiance and Canyon de Chelly, I think they must be Hopi. They are real people, like us, but live like the Tanoan and Zuni Pueblo nations, in pueblo villages on top of buttes or mesas so that nobody can kill them in their sleep after they have worked in their fields down below. I have never been able to understand how real people would want to be *farmers*!"

Doc Frank repeated his remarks about location and suggested a band of Hopi, drifting north from their somewhat crowded Black Mesa Reserve to live free of B.I.A. meddling like the ancient cliff dwellers.

Agent Thalmann got highly pissed and demanded to know where a damned Jew got off calling him a meddler. Things were really going swell before they were halfway down to Fort Defiance, and as Longarm gently but firmly reminded them, they still had to backtrack to that unmapped canyon with *Navaho* guides once they got to Fort Defiance, if they ever did at the rate they were going.

Longarm thought when he chided the bickering leaders about their childish ways that internal strife was their main worry. For nothing had come at them from *outside* since they'd left Animas Point and so, if that so-called reporter had been in cahoots with the late Jed Farnsworth. a.k.a. Pecos Moran, they'd lost the rascal somewhere behind them. Grover pointed out *he* hadn't expected them to veer off the main route to Fort Defiance. So it was sort of comical to consider the poor plotter tracking them down the wrong and way-longer trail, until you studied on why the hell he and Farnsworth had been after "Buck Crawford" to begin with. Nobody but Longarm had caught the fake ranger's slip in a haunted whorehouse that hadn't seemed haunted.

But as others had found out to their sorrow in the Four Corners country, the dramatic scenery was more dangerous than it looked. It was late afternoon, and they were riding across the dead flat top of a mesa betwixt the canyon they'd left at noon and another Towasi hoped to make before sundown when Sergeant Wynn, riding out to one side a short ways, flushed a deer fawn that had been playing possom in a nest of sage, like its momma had told it to.

But the fawn was at that stage where one begins to doubt one's parents, or smart enough to see you could only play possom up to a sensible point. So it sprang to its wiry legs to bound off across the sage into the sunset as Wynn spurred after it, whooping, "Hot damn! Venison for supper!" as he drew his saddle gun at full gallop.

Tosawi screamed, *"Kanniti! En tzareno maruhkat nukusi!"*—too upset to warn Wynn in English. So Longarm yelled, "Let it go, Sarge! He wants us to stick to this trail!"

Then the deer fawn was bobbing alone into the sunset as Wynn and his mount simply vanished from sight.

Longarm reined in to mutter, "Shit!" as the lieutenant shouted in confusion, "What happened? Where did Wynn go?"

Longarm tethered his own mount to a sage clump as he waited for the others to join them. Then he said, "Don't nobody ride out yonder! Like Tosawi just tried to warn 'em, the sarge and his mule just fell into the pumpkin!"

Chapter 16

As Longarm eased gingerly on foot through thigh-high sagebrush, that deer fawn was still bounding as a distant dot into the red, gold and purple clouds of sundown. Longarm could see how a critter crossing familiar range could have simply bounded across the cleft and the mule might have managed as well, had not the confused stake man reined in to throw it off stride at just the wrong time.

He eased over to what seemed a beaten path through the sage from north to south and dropped to his hands and knees to crawl on and peer down into the blackness, calling out, "Sergeant Wynn?"

His own voice echoed some. That was the only sound from the depths. By now the others had joined him, save for the Indian kids holding the mules. Nobody was as close to the edge as Longarm, who called back to Doc Frank, "How far can a man and mule fall without dying for certain, Doc?"

Frank said, "It so happens some English doctors experimented, with animals, not people, of course. A mouse you can drop down a thousand foot mine shaft, and it will get up and walk away. A cat won't, but the results are not so messy. A dog? Messy. A mine donkey? Don't ask! Is donkey soup a clear enough picture?"

Longarm said, "Forget that mule, then. What about Wynn?"

Frank said, "Twenty feet, maybe something broken, even his neck, but the chances are good. Forty feet, he might just make it if we got him to a hospital and in traction. A lot of traction. Sixty feet? He's dead, even if he's still breathing."

Longarm asked Tosawi how deep the cleft was. The Indian said he didn't know and suggested anything from thirty feet to three thousand. Longarm said, "I got a forty-foot throw-rope on my stock-saddle. I could use something longer. Could you manage sixty or seventy feet for me, pard?"

The Indian called out to one of his helpers. Agent Thalmann asked, "What's the point? You just heard Frank say he's probably dead!"

Longarm rose, muttering, "How do you stand not hugging yourself to death for being such a swell cuss, Marty?"

Frank said, "We need more rope. I'm going down with you."

Longarm replied, "I dunno, Doc. No offense, but I'm younger than you and have you ever done much rock climbing?"

Frank said, "No. Have you splinted many broken bones or lifted a man with a broken back without killing him?"

Longarm cast aside his hat, jacket and gunbelt as he soberly said, "I follow your drift, Doc. But I hope you understand the risk we'll both be taking!"

Frank shrugged and asked, "You expected to get out of this world alive? It's risk, risk, risk already from first breath to last, confidential. As a doctor, I *know*. So where's all that rope already?"

The Indians produced two seventy-five foot hemp tether

lines as Tosawi had commanded and drove tent pegs deep, well back from the rim, before dropping the loose coils down and then down some more into the darkness, ink-black darkness at this hour, thanks to that red western sky. Longarm picked up the slack of one as he said, "*Bueno*, we go down side by side with our backs to the far wall, our feet braced against the near wall, with the dangle betwixt our thighs and our hands above us, holding on like hell, but trying to hold most of our weight with the friction betwixt sandstone, shirts and shoe leather."

Frank said, "Nu, who's arguing?" as Fiona cried out, "Don't do it! I don't want to lose either one of you!"

They both started down, of course, as Fiona pissed and moaned above them, and Wilma Thalmann yelled at her to be still and let her—dammit—*listen*!

Longarm grunted, "I hate to say it, but at the moment Miss Wilma makes more sense."

Frank grunted, "Fiona can get exited, as you seem to have noticed. There are questions a gentleman never asks, but if I wasn't a gentleman, I'd sure like to ask some."

Longarm growled, "Since there are questions no gentleman asks and answers no gentleman would give if he was asked 'em, I reckon you'll just never know, will you, Doc? Hold the thought, and keep it down to a roar. We're supposed to be listening for signs of life, not gossiping like biddy hens!"

They worked their way further down, then down some more, pausing every few feet to call to Wynn in the pitch blackness.

When Frank hissed, "Listen! Did you hear that?" Longarm nodded and called out, "Hey, Sarge?"

An ominously distant voice called back, "Where the fuck am I?"

Longarm called, "You fell into the pumpkin. How bad are you hurt?"

There came a long silence. Then the man wedged far

143

below managed, "Bad. I think I busted my back. I can't feel shit from my rib cage down. I can't move my arms, but they both hurt like hell, so they got to be wedged against me by the fucking rock to either side. I don't see how you're ever going to get me out, Crawford."

Doc Frank called down, "Are you upright, facedown, faceup, or what?" He added in a whispered aside, "He wouldn't be conscious if he was head down, and, confidential, I'm running out of rope already!"

Longarm muttered, "Shit, me, too. I thought you said nobody could fall more than sixty feet and live, Doc."

Frank said, "Sixty feet kersplatt they can't. If he's wedged in a sort of funnel, it's possible. But what am I saying? If he's talking he's alive, so what do we do now?"

Longarm said, "We need more rope." Then he called up, "Hey, Tosawi? Can you rustle up more rope, say a hundred and fifty feet and drop it down alongside this one?"

The Indian called back he'd try. Longarm called down to Wynn to advise him of the situation. They received no answer. He called down again. Frank said, "He's unconscious, or dead. Think the reverse of a crucifixion with the same results. Arms pulling the rib cage wide or compressing it too tightly and, either way, you can't breathe so good, even without a spinal fracture!"

When Tosawi's head popped over the rim again, outline against a purple slit of sky, he yelled down, "No more rope! Climb those ropes you have! *Ekakwitzet* to west, now *Paa'ema* coming *this* way!"

Longarm said, "Oh, shit, he's talking about flash flooding! I thought it might be clouding up in the west! We got to get out of here, Doc!"

They started climbing as, above them, Tosawi urged them higher.

Then, from the dark depths below, they heard a mournful croaking cry, and Frank sobbed, "He's still alive! We have to go back down!"

Longarm said, "No, we don't. We don't have any way to reach him in time. If we don't keep climbing we'll just die along with him, Doc!"

Frank froze in place, insisting, "You go on! I can't! I won't! I am a doctor! It's my sworn duty as a doctor and a *tzedakah* of my faith, I can't let another die through my own inaction!"

Longarm called up, "Hey, Tosawi? I want your young men to grab hold this one rope and start pulling. Tie your end to my saddle horn if you have to. Just pull like hell 'til I tell you to stop!"

Then he looped the slack below his grip around the both of them and when Frank tried to pull free Longarm said, "You're going up with me if I have to drag you by that beard. So what's it going to be, Doc?"

Frank swore he'd never forgive Longarm as the two of them began to rise without effort. Before Longarm could say he didn't give a shit, the cleft they were rising from was filled with a thunderous roar and when Frank asked what on earth that could be, Longarm dryly remarked, "*Yaponcha.* Some see him as a rain god. Some see him as the thunderbird. Either way, it's raining somewhere that's drained by this slot and, oh boy! Here she comes!"

But they were well above the flood level as the darkness all around filled with continuous thunder and rising mist, and the Indians soon had them out of the slot, panting prone on the ground under a balmy gloaming sky with just an occasional flash of silent lighting off to the west.

Doc Frank was crying. Lieutenant Grover came over to hunker down beside them and ask about Wynn. Frank sniffed, took a deep breath and said, "There was nothing we could do for him," which was the simple truth when you studied on it.

As Longarm helped Frank to his feet, Fiona stamped

her feet and said she was cross with both of them, so there. Old Tosawi came over to them, coiling rope hand over hand. He stopped to stare stone-faced at the doc as he told Longarm, "Hear me, this one is not yet *saltu ka saltu*, but I think he is a real person."

"He has a good heart," Longarm gravely agreed.

Doc Frank suddenly laughed and said, "Aw, mush!" so they shook on it, and Frank asked whether the remains of Wynn and his mule might wash out into the canyon ahead.

Longarm said, "Not in any shape you'd want to look at, Doc. All that water-carved and pumpkin-colored sandstone is pretty to look at but it's gritty as sandpaper."

In the end, they never found but a single trace of Sergeant Wynn. They camped for the night where they were, relying on their water bags and burning sagebrush. Then they rode on and down into the wider canyon ahead, where they found themselves following a brawling muddy creek to the south, with the rainwater already subsiding. It was during a trail break that Fiona, heeding a call to nature in a clump of willow spotted something out on a sandbar and called Longarm's attention to it when she rejoined the others smoking and jawing in the shade of the eastern wall of the canyon.

Longarm, Lieutenant Grover and the doc moved upstream and out across the shallows to where an army boot lay lonesome, like the leftover paw of a mouse some awfully big cat had et. Doc Frank gingerly bent to stand the boot up and peek inside. He grimaced and said, "Yes. His foot's still in it. Do we bury it or take it with us?"

"In this heat we'd better bury it," said Longarm, adding, "Ain't about to do him any good, but I'd feel better if we had us a sky pilot along to say a few words."

Doc Frank didn't say anything until Tosawi joined them as they carried the boot over to dry ground and said he'd have his boys dig a grave for it. The doc went on to his tethered mule to get something from his saddlebags.

146

Nobody paid attention until the hole was down to the water table and Longarm agreed with Tosawi that was deep as it needed to be. That was when they saw Doc Frank had thrown a white wool shawl around his shoulders and lashed a sort of bitty black box to his forehead. The lieutenant laughed. Longarm said, "Don't. I've been to Jew funerals. I know what he's doing."

So they all stood respectfully as Doc Frank read from his pocket Torah, selecting that psalm about walking through the valley of death that his folk and doubtless Sergeant Wynn's agreed upon.

Fiona, standing next to Longarm, began to cry and even the bitchy Wilma had the good grace to look sort of sad.

Then it came time to ride on. So they did, leaving an improvised cross on the rocks piled over the sergeant's foot. The cross had been Fiona's notion. The more practical rocks had been suggested by Longarm lest coyotes paw the boot out of the sand below.

They spent that whole day in that one long twisty canyon, more than once spotting sign that told of other white riders using the same northsouth route. At natural trail breaks the tin cans, cigar butts and such could have been read as evidence of army columns on the march. But Tosawi and Longarm agreed they were about as big a bunch as that shorter unmapped route could support. The freshly reflooded creek had already subsided to scattered pools along a drying streak of mudflats and, without being told, Tosawi's Indian help had taken to swinging down from their saddles to gather up such deadwood as they spotted in passing, since it lay nowhere in abundance and they'd need some, come the end of the day on the trail.

They got to where Tosawi had chosen in advance a good night camp, following the west wall in the afternoon shade of the same. So they might have missed the cliff dwellings above had not Fiona pointed at some busted up

Indian pottery on the gravel ahead. A heap of busted up Indian pottery.

Tosawi, who'd apparantly decided Fiona was a person, too, and hence started to call her little sister, said, "*Taibo* break pottery a lot. Nobody knows why. They like to write their names all over things, too. They are like children."

Fiona looked up to barely make out from that angle a freestone corner of one building. "Ooh, there's a pueblo on a ledge up there!"

So as the Indians set up the camp, Longarm led Fiona, Lieutenant Grover and the doc up there, lest they break their fool necks. Tosawi said he had no call to visit the Hohokum. Neither Wilma nor Agent Thalmann chose to tag along. For a man out to establish his own Indian agency, Thalmann didn't seem all that interested in Indians.

Longarm warned the others not to trust any wooden ladders, really notched logs, because they were likely hundreds of years old and inclined to turn to punk under you at awkward times. It was tougher but safer to use such handholds and toeholds as there might be.

Sister Fiona seemed agile as everyone else despite her skirts and they soon made it up to the ruins, to wish they hadn't, as soon as they'd looked around a mite.

Tosawi's point about white vandals had been well taken. For some reason known only to little boys and a certain class of grown men, a heap of effort had gone into inscribing "Fuck You" or "Jake Sucks" in charcoal on the highest wall in sight. The likely one-clan compound of quarters, graneries and prayer kivas had never been too big to begin with, and cleverly-fitted but mortarless stone walls were all too easy to tear down, for whatever reason. They found nothing of further interest in any of the busted open chambers. Anything that hadn't just been tossed over the side had been carried away. Lieutenant Grover darkly muttered, "Civilians!" and Fiona asked, "Why?"

Longarm shrugged and suggested, "We're following one of them outlaw trails you hear so much about. Outlaws by definition are hardly responsible citizens. Albeit I've seen where wagon trains of folk not wanted by the law have carved their names all over a chimney rock, as if anybody else was ever going to care they'd passed that way." •

Chapter 17

The next afternoon Tosawi led them through a natural arch into another canyon when the one they'd been following veered west to aim for the jumble of canyons known as the *Grand* one. An earlier traveler had taken time and effort to let it be known that Malo Bill had been there and thought Nolan was a fag.

They camped the next night on higher ground hugging the western wall, and since earlier riders hadn't wanted to drown in their sleep, either, there were now empty cans, paper wrappings and a dirty picture book to be kicked downslope to clear the site for tidier folk. The night fires were smaller, and the night watch was tight that night, now that it was obvious they were on an outlaw trail.

Longarm didn't think he was revealing too much about his true ID when he explained to his dudes how western outlaws rode far and wide betwixt robberies to take advantage of thinly spread lawmen in a land of conflicting jurisdictions. The James-Younger gang, alone, were known to have ranged from the Great Lakes to the Dakota Territory in the north and as far south as Texas, and they were considered home boys.

He opined, "An old boy stopping a Butterfield stage in

Apache Pass to the south could be robbing the Union Pacific to the north by the time the Arizona posse quit looking for him in all the wrong places. As you can see for your own selves, we ain't passed through a town or even a homestead in many a day."

The next day they broke trail near a looted and vandalized cliff dwelling. Late that afternoon, riding point with old Tosawi and the lieutenant, Longarm spotted a row of what he took at first for wall-to-wall scarecrows across the canyon and declared, "Now this is just plain chickenshit!" as they rode close enough to see what someone had done with mummified cliff dwellers from back up the canyon a ways.

The long dead Hohokum or Anasazi, depending, had been laid to rest in fetal positions wrapped in robes woven with yucca fibers and wild turkey feathers. Left to their druthers in dry caves way up high, a dried out Indian could last indefinite. Stuck in grotesque upright positions like horrid lollipops on sticks shoved up their dried out dead asses, they were commencing to fall apart in the damper air of the canyon floor.

As the rest of the part caught up, Longarm and Grover had just agreed it was more practical to bury them nearby than scout for the clefts the vandals had hauled them out of.

Agent Thalmann snapped, "We don't have time to keep burying bits and pieces of people, damn it! I have to get to my new post as the Chindi agent!"

Longarm said, "Shut up. I ain't gonna say that again. These are human remains we're talking about and I say we give 'em a decent burial before we do shit about your agency. Sorry, ladies."

As the Indians, in fact, buried the long dead strangers they described in Ho as "people all used up," Doc Frank said a prayer in Hebrew for them, and old Tosawi chanted them on their way to wherever dead folk went. Quill Indians were less certain than missionaries who had it all down on paper. Having only oral traditions to go by, the differant bands of various nations tended to get such advice as their own medicine man recalled from his own earlier instructions. So books written about *the* noble savage religion tended to read sort of silly to anyone who'd ever spent much time with more than one Indian.

Once they'd buried the long dead Hohokum, they rode on a few more miles to make what Tosawi promised would be their next to last such stop. He said they'd be leaving the outlaw trail to rejoin the more well-known if longer military trace, an easy two day's ride on.

In the night, standing picket, Longarm overheard some mighty hard words from the larger tent shared by the Thalmanns. Longarm knew it was none of his beeswax but since he had nothing better to listen to in the dark but crickets, he drifted closer to hear the pompous agent describing his woman as a fucking slut.

To which Wilma Thalmann replied in a tone dulcet as oil of vitriol, "At least I can still manage to fuck! Which is more than can be said for some old farts I know!"

So Longarm eased away, whistling under his breath as, once again, old Wilma had topped his expectations after he'd *allowed* she was a *bitch*!

It was a caution how some men put up with women like that. Unless old Wilma was fibbing to a man in a position to know, Agent Thalmann wasn't getting any. So how come he put up with her shit?

Another day and night through nowheres much got them into reservation lands the Navaho took more serious, betwixt the Pueblo Colorado to the west and Fort Defiance on the new Arizona-New Mexico line. So now they were riding where merino sheep grazed every rise too steep to drill in beans, corn, peppers, squash or tobacco. Fiona opined the Navaho hogans they kept passing reminded her of Eskimo snow houses, albeit made of mud, sticks and sagebrush thatch. The Navaho all around kept any opinions they'd formed about Fiona or anyone else to their own selves.

They got to Fort Defiance just after the afternoon retreat formation to be welcomed by a silver-haired and silver-oak-leafed Lieutenant Colonel Wurtz, commanding a skeletonized cav, skimmed of its cream to beef up Fort Apache and other outposts closer to the action along the border that summer, with Victorio at it again.

As its name indicated, Fort Defiance had been built in defiance of undefeated war chiefs who'd warned the blue sleeves not to do that in the middle of their hunting grounds. But now that the way-chanters were asking Changing Woman for rain instead of victory, Fort Defiance was a shadow of its former self, albeit even Tosawi and his younger Utes would get to sleep under roofs that evening.

The setup reminded Longarm of Fort Sumner on the Pecos, built to control Quill Indians, then sold as surplus property to the Anglo-Mex Maxwell clan to become their private enclave. It cost money to run an army post, whether there was need for one or not.

That evening after they'd run the flag down to the bugle call of retreat, Colonel Wurtz invited all but the Indians to the officers' club to jaw about their future plans and see what he might do to assist in the same.

He got less smiley-faced as Agent Thalmann explained how he meant to register, vaccinate and civilize all those Chindi running loose somewhere betwixt where they were and the old Navaho stronghold of Canyon de Chelly.

The aged-in-the-saddle cavalry officer snapped, "Damn it! Sorry, ladies, I thought we had that settled with you B.I.A. boys. *Chindi* means "ghost" in Navaho. There are no Chindi Indians. There are scared or wicked Navaho shepherd boys who've been scaring the littler kids with ghost stories. My troopers and I don't just sit on our hands out here, you know. We run patrols to show the flag and remind the Navaho we're keeping an eye on them. There aren't any other Indians in this area. It's all Navaho reservation. In spite of all their weeping and wailing, Congress in its wisdom set aside a hundred times as much federal land for the Navaho than it ever gave the far more sensible Pueblo, who've yet to take the war path since we took these territories from Mexico."

Thalmann said he still meant to establish a Chindi agency, carved out of Navaho reserves, once he found out where in thunder they were.

Lieutenant Grover produced the survey chart he'd been making notes on in pencil as he soothed, "I'm sure the captain must know better than we where the Navaho say they've encountered these mysterious Chindi Indians."

He spread the map across the bare dining table they'd been sharing as he explained those penciled *X* marks indicated navigational calculations he'd made along that unmapped outlaw trail with the aid of his compass and sextant.

Wurtz studied the map with some interest before he asked, "You say there's a beaten path over this way, where the chart's so blank?"

He stabbed a finger to the chart paper to continue, "All, right, this is where we are right now. You can see where the Hubbell Trading Post lies, *here*. I've never asked a superstitious Navaho to indicate on any map where he says he saw a ghost. But most of the reports seem to come from around *here*, northwest of the trading post. Hubbell is not *supposed* to sell them liquor, but they must be drinking something mighty strong."

Grover frowned down at the map to decide, "Didn't we see something like white construction on the far side of that ravine Tosawi led us along this afternoon? He said it was out of our way, and there was nothing there of interest."

Doc Frank said, "Nu, what would a Ute find interesting about a Navaho trading post? All our Indians have been on edge since we started passing Navaho in the distance this afternoon."

Agent Thalmann decided he needed a Navaho guide to lead the way to his new agency.

It was Longarm who said with a weary smile, "No, you don't, Marty. We know the way. We've been that way. Can't you read maps?"

Lieutenant Grover stared soberly down at his own pencil marks to marvel, "I see what you mean, Buck! If Navaho have reported their mysterious Chindi north of *here*, and that camel rock I noted this morning was *here*, we'd have ridden *through* that canyon the Chindi are said to inhabit!"

"That's ridiculous!" Thalmann protested, "There were no Indians of any sort in any of those canyons Tosawi led us through on our way down here!"

Longarm said, "You're wrong. There were Indians in more than one of them uncharted canyons. They just happened to have died a few hundred years ago."

Doc Frank gasped, "Of course! Those mummified cliff dwellers! On sticks like lollipops yet and would *you* like to herd your sheep around a corner to see them grinning at you all in a row?"

Lieutenant Grover laughed and said, "I'd run all the way home and tell my momma I'd just met up with bogeymen, or *chindi*, if I was speaking to her in Navaho!"

Agent Thalmann was looking green around the gills as Longarm told him, "There you go, Marty. White outlaws using them side canyons as a private right-of-way set them really spooky scarecrows up to keep it private, knowing how most Indians feel about haunts. Not knowing exactly what some few Navaho had really seen, somebody sent in a report about them complaining about *chindi*. It's always a good notion to keep track of Indian complaints. Nobody was lying on purpose. The tale just got scrambled in transmission. There ain't no Chindi Indian tribe. We've been sent on a snipe hunt, and come all this way at the cost of Sergeant Wynn's life for *nothing!*"

Wilma Thalmann, who'd been seated at the next table with Fiona, got to her feet triumphanty to announce, "I told you you were a fool, Martin Luther Thalmann! After seeing all I ever want to see of this harsh and barren land, I'm *glad* we won't be stuck out here! So now I'm going to bed, and I don't want to be disturbed, you silly, silly little man!"

She marched off toward the empty barracks the captain's orderly had shown them to, earlier. Fiona allowed she was feeling tuckered, too, and rose to leave with a meaningful glance at Longarm.

He was stuck there long enough to convince everyone but Thalmann of his simple solution to the mystery of the mystery tribe. It took him 'til after they'd blown taps, or lights out, to rejoin Fiona in the former NCO quarters at one end of the deserted barracks. Wilma Thalmann had claimed the similar private chamber at the far end, with long rows of bare bedsteads between. Longarm and Fiona neither knew nor cared where Agent Thalmann meant to spend the night.

Fiona said she meant to give Longarm a night to remember, since it wasn't too clear how many more they might have together before she had to head back East with Doc Frank after donating all their medical supplies to the Navaho Agency to save on freight charges and bother.

But, lucky for all concerned, Longarm had just hung his gun-rig on the bedpost and still had his boots and jeans on when all hell busted loose outside!

Grabbing his .44-40 from its holster, he warned Fiona to stay put and ducked out to run the length of the empty barracks in response to the fusillade of five shots. As the door at the far end popped open, he warned the dim figure emerging from Wilma Thalmann's chosen room to drop that gun and grab for the rafters.

When that didn't work he pistol-whupped the cuss flat and stepped over him into the smoke-filled darkness to light a waxed Mex match with his free hand.

Wilma Thalmann lay faceup across the bed without a stitch of clothes or a sign of life. She'd sure been a hairy little thing, and her tits had been grand before they'd been shot up that way.

Lieutenant Grover lay curled up like a cat on the rug between her bare feet, just as naked and just as dead. Some of those bullets old Wilma had taken in her breast had gone through Grover's back and out his front along the way. There would have been more blood had not both their hearts been stopped so sudden.

Still holding the candlelike waterproof match aloft, Longarm turned to see he'd guessed right about the poor bastard he'd knocked cold.

Down at the far end, Fiona was calling, "What happened? I want to see!"

Longarm called back, "No you don't. They don't need a nurse and you want to get dressed sudden. Old Martin Luther just caught his wife in bed with Lieutenant Grover, and she was lying when she told me they had an understanding about such matters!"

Chapter 18

Once they'd patched Thalmann's split scalp and locked him up in the guard house, the white survivors of the comedy of errors were sitting with Colonel Wurtz in his private quarters, with the motherly Miss Aurora, his wife, keeping everyone's coffee mugs full as she puttered back and forth.

The colonel agreed with "Buck Crawford"—neither Fiona nor Doc Frank were in any trouble, save for being a long way from home for no good reason and facing the pending courtmartial of Agent Thalmann as material witnesses. Thalmann had been yelling dumb things about not being subject to a military trial after gunning two people, including a U.S. Army officer on a military post, established, for Gawd's sake, as early as 1850 in defiance of the once meaner Navaho.

Longarm had no call to show off. So he never mentioned that time a civilian couple had driven on to the San Francisco Presidio for some slap and tickle, resulting in a court-martial for rape, punishable by death, when the gal was only trying to get her swain to marry up with her by filing those charges.

Fiona and the doc both knew how Wilma Thalmann

had been screwing around and stood ready to swear "Buck Crawford" had no ulterior cause to pistol-whip the outraged husband after he'd gunned his wife and her lover. When Fiona said she felt sorry for the poor simp, the colonel allowed they'd likely let him off with some time in Jefferson Barracks to meditate upon his shortcomings as a husband, or a man of common sense. Longarm waited until they'd all yawned some and rose to call it a night before he told Fiona he'd be along in a minute and took Colonel Wurtz aside, muttering, "It's time to spread some cards faceup on the table, Colonel."

Wurtz suggested they stroll down to the end of the veranda where they could smoke in private. Once they had, Longarm told the colonel, "My name aint Buck Crawford. I'm Deputy U.S. Marshal Custis Long of the Denver District Court, on special assignment, undercover, with the approval of the powers that be."

Wurtz stuck out a hand to say, "I've heard of you, Longarm. What's the real story about that killing, this evening?"

Longarm said, "There's no mystery, there. As we established inside just now, Thalmann was an asshole and his wife was a two-faced two-timing bitch he should have shot long ere this. That young shavetail deserved better, but when you cornhole married women, you ought to know there's some risk involved. I was only sent to tag along with the fools errand just ended as an excuse to investigate more mysterious doings up the far side of the San Juan. But I'd have never seen what I now suspect as some answers had not I ridden all the way down this way to view both ends of that unmapped outlaw trail we've been talking about."

"You mean a sneaky series of shortcuts through at least one canyon haunted by ghostly Indians?" the colonel nodded.

Longarm said, "I do. In my six or eight years riding

for Justice, I have seen how crooks tend to repeat tricks over and over, once they come up with one that seems to work. Somebody wanting to keep the south end of their secret trail a secret has been scaring off stray Navaho with a haunted canyon. Mummified scarecrows and likely shots across the bows of any sheep coming up the canyon floodplain. Can't be hard to scare a shepherd boy who's already edgy about haunts, or *chindis*."

Longarm got both their smokes lit as he added, "At the *north* end of the same beaten outlaw path lies a haunted whorehouse, where white riders instead of Indian shepherds keep seeing notorious dead folk, unless, of course, they show up with a badge and a search warrant. See what I mean about similar patterns?"

The colonel nodded gravely and replied, "They don't want anyone else to know about that secret shorter route. So they've been scaring off possible trespassers at either end and . . . Hold on, how scared off would you call a lawman with a search warrant?"

Longarm shook his head and said, "It ain't that simple. The whorehouse in question is a hard ride north of the shorter route old Tosawi led us to. He says it was a war trail before it became an outlaw trail. Either way, owlhoot riders popping out the north end are way more anxious for a place to hole up and lay low as they decide whether it might be safe to ride on up to Durango along a public thoroughfare. I suspect someone's running a sort of hotel for outlaws in Animas Point."

"In a haunted whorehouse?" Wurtz frowned.

Longarm shook his head and said, "Stage magicians *misdirect* their audience to study on something flashy as they quietly slip a rabbit into their hat with the other hand. One naked lady covered with a mess of black rubber spiders looks much like another who might've died in Brooklyn and, hell, leave us not bother to count the ways mortal pimps and whores could be gussied up to pass for wilder folk to gossip about. The simple *motive* would be bait on the outskirts of town for any visiting lawman to sniff around, whilst announcing his visit to town. Owlhoot riders laying over in less interesting digs, closer to sudden tranportation, would know when it came time to clear the streets and lay doggo 'til the law grew weary of shithouse rumors and moved on, satisfied there were no haunts in that whorehouse and never even considering half a dozen boarded up establishments of some size right there in town!"

Colonel Wurtz said, "That works for me, Longarm. How can I help you out with your . . . misdirection?"

Longarm said, "For openers, you might excuse me as a witness, seeing there's no mystery about who shot whom, down here, this evening."

When Wurtz said, "Done. I'm sure we can manage with just depositions and his signed confession, once I have a serious talk with him, alone. Is that it?"

Longarm said, "Not quite. If your army telegraph wire patches in to the Western Union web, I got more than one wire to send before I ride out alone, before dawn. I'll tell you, as a pal, I mean to drift into Animas Point unannounced and see if I meet up with any haunts. But I'd be obliged if you didn't tell anybody else, not even Doc Frank or Sister Fiona about this conversation."

Wurtz said should anybody ask, he'd have no idea where that Crawford cuss had gone. So they shook on it and Longarm went across the parade to those NCO quarters to part friendly with the chestnut-haired Fiona.

Thus it came to pass that about the time Fiona and Doc Frank had made it halfway north along the regular route, Longarm rode into Animas Point alone, hoping old Tosawi and those Indians kids had made it home without his guidance. He'd borrowed an army mule for his own use, so Tosawi would only have to account for the loss of that one Spanish saddle mule on his own journey north.

As he unsaddled his jaded mount at the municipal corral in Animas Point, old Stubby Croft, the town law, ambled over to howdy him, saying, "Thought you'd be down to Fort Defiance with them other B.I.A. folk, Crawford."

Longarm draped the saddle over a corral pole and removed his own bridle from the government mount's muzzle as he said, "Ain't working for the B.I.A. no more. Things went to hell in a hack, and I lit out on my own when they wanted me to testify at a fucking trial about a cheating wife and her mortified husband."

He draped the bridle over the horn of his borrowed rope and heaved the whole load atop one shoulder as he added, "I had no part in the mess, and with the man who was supposed to pay me locked away in the guardhouse I felt no call to hang around. So here I am and now I got to get it on back to your only hotel."

The town law fell in step with him as he quietly asked, "Are you sure that's where you want to hole up, Buck? That mule you rode in on wears a U.S. Army brand, and, well, that one hotel everybody knows about ain't exactly the only hotel in town."

Longarm pretended not to care as he trudged on, replying, "Do tell? How much might they charge at any other hotels here in town, Snuffy?"

The older man asked, "How does ten dollars a night with wine, women and song throwed in?"

Longarm laughed incredulously and demanded, "Who do I look like to you Animas Point boys, Bet-a-Million Gates, the bobwire king?"

Stubby Croft said, "Nope. More like a man on the run from the provost marshal's office. We got a wire about you, days ago, from Fort Defiance. Seems you lit out on them after you'd been served as a material witness, and they're mad as hell about it."

Longarm shrugged his free shoulder and said, "Aw, shit, I ain't the one on trial. They'll get over me and their

163

mule leaving a mite early. Even if they don't, I could never afford ten dollars a day for enough days to matter."

He let that sink in before he added, "Not unless I wired home for money. But the last time I had to do that they made me promise not to do that no more."

Stubby Croft said, "Suit yourself. You know best how bad they want you. You know where to find me, should you want me for anything."

Longarm moved on, trying not to grin too wolfishly as he gave the old-timer more rope to hang himself. Things were starting to make more sense. There'd of course been no way to switch a whorehouse back and forth from sordid to eerie without the town law noticing and those mortal-looking whores had addressed Stubby by his nickname when he'd responded to that gunplay out yonder.

Longarm hoped nobody out yonder had picked up on that slip of the tongue that had led to his shoot-out with the fake ranger who'd somehow figured out who he was. But Longarm was all too aware of how thin the ice he was skating on might be as he checked his saddle and shit into that same hotel room and headed over to that big saloon to rinse some trail dust out of his mouth and see if anybody else in town had anything to say about that army mule he'd ridden in on.

He thought he was ready for most anything Animas Point had to throw at him as he strode through the batwings into the dimmer light between the entrance and the long, nearly-deserted bar. Those same regulars were at their eternal penny-ante game in a far corner. A lean and sort of hungry looking rider with a hatchet face lounged halfway along the bar, nursing a scuttle of beer and a fifth of bourbon at his elbow on the zinc. Longarm had never laid eyes on him before. So it was just as well he'd palmed his double derringer before striding into such uncertain surroundings. For he'd have never beaten the son of a bitch to the draw when the stranger slapped leather at the sight of him!

The bitty belly-gun in Longarm's big fist barked twice ere the stranger's Schofield cleared its tied-down holster, and, as Longarm dropped the empty derringer to the sawdust and drew his own six-gun, they could both see it was over.

"Gawd . . . damn . . . you're good!" sighed the stranger in a surprisingly fatalistic tone before he dropped his own gun, tried to make it to the nearest chair, and collapsed to the same sawdust, limp as a wet rag doll.

Longarm hunkered down, six-gun in hand, to pick up and pocket his empty derringer as he quietly asked, "Any of you other gents have a stake in this game?"

The barkeep stood back up to declare, "None of us here knew either one of you, Mister. That poor cuss on the floor is all yours to keep and cherish!"

Longarm wasn't surpised to be joined by Stubby Croft and two of his deputies within minutes. As Longarm put his six-gun away and proceeded to reload his derringer with loose rounds from a jacket pocket, he calmly told the town law, "Same deal as out to that whorehouse. Ask these other gents if he didn't draw first. But don't expect this child to tell you why!"

Stubby Croft said, "These other gents will tell me most anything I tell them I want to hear, Mr. Crawford. I suspect you're going to want to wire home for money, now, right?"

To which Longarm could only reply, "I reckon."

Leaving his deputies to tidy up at the saloon, Stubby Croft walked Longarm to the Western Union so's he could wire "Buck Crawford's kin" in Denver.

Knowing the older lawman might read the message, and not knowing who Stubby or most anyone else in Animas Point might know in Denver, the undercover lawman addressed his plea to a certain friendly mine-owning widow woman who dwelt just down Sherman Street from the Vails. Longarm knew his unexpected telegram was certain to surprise the shit out of her, but she was a smart old gal, and, with any luck, she'd know who he meant when he asked her to scout up his "Uncle Billy" and tell him he needed money bad, citing an early little jam he'd gotten himself into down Brownsville way. Longarm knew she'd have no idea what he meant, but old Billy Vail might recall the case and how they'd worked things out. Any fancier attempt at confidential code would be asking for trouble that wasn't worth the ante. He was mildy surprised and more than a little chagrined when Stubby never asked to see the form before Longarm handed it across the counter to the Western Union clerk.

It was possible, but unlikely, the clerk would show the town law a copy of his message, later. The nationwide telegraph outfit offered top dollar for telegraphers, and employees who betrayed the trust of a paying customer were fired and then blacklisted so's they'd play hell ever dotting a dash again.

Back outside on the walk, Longarm allowed he'd wait at the hotel 'til his kin sent some jingle for that *other* . . . hotel.

The town law of Animas Point demurred, "You'd best come right along with me so's we can get you off the streets and out of sight before words speads about your latest shooting. That's the second man you've shot in your two known visits to this town. What makes you so mean, old son?"

Longarm soberly replied, "I'm still working on why either one of 'em was out to clean my plow. Are you saying you and your pals are willing to trust me until I get some money from home?"

Stubby Croft replied, easily, "Why not, old son? You

166

could be in a lot of trouble if we don't hide you good and soon. You'll be in way more trouble if it turns out you are not to be trusted for your room and board at the opera house!"

Chapter 19

Longarm wanted to kick himself the minute Stubby Croft mentioned the fool opera house. For it stood smack in the center of town. He was a lawman who'd been told something sneaky was going on there in Animas Point. Yet he'd stood out front of the boarded-up property with Fiona and Doc Frank feeling sorry for the owner of the shut down pile!

He didn't ask the town law who owned the better part of a business block in the center of town. The deed would be a matter of public record at the county seat, a tediouus ride back along the Animas. The county sheriff seized and auctioned off property no taxes were being paid on, boarded-up or otherwise.

Since it was listed on the tax rolls as vacant property, assessed at the little more than the original value of the vacant lot, there'd be no call for anyone from the county seat to inspect the old opera house, whilst nobody there in Animas Point would have any right or sensible reason to! As Stubby led him around to the stage entrance off a blind alley, Longarm recalled from having toured with the Divine Sarah Bernhardt, guarding a national treasure of France for the State Department, how many dressing rooms, green rooms, prop rooms and other hidey-holes you'd find backstage in even a modest opera house. So he wasn't too surprised when Stubby introduced him just inside the stage door to another older gent described as the watchman. Stubby told the other old cuss, who answered to Pops Grenoble, how Buck's room and board was on the cuff, for the time being. Pops didn't ask how come. So Longarm knew he was lower on the totem pole.

Stubby Croft, who had to be higher, told Longarm he'd be back to help him cash that money order when it came in. After he'd left, the cuss guarding the one unlocked and out-of-the-way entrance let out a whoop for a Claudine, a waiflike brunette who could have passed for fourteen until you looked into her eyes, who emerged from the backstage gloom to show "Buck Crawford" up to his new quarters.

They weren't bad. The former dressing room was illuminated by an overhead skylight and surprisingly well furnished with mismatched but fairly expensive looking furniture, consisting of a dresser, wardrobe, two upholstered chairs as didn't match and a big brass bedstead. The corner sink had running water, cold, from both taps.

Claudine said he'd be served his supper in the room in less than an hour and told him to summon her for anything else he needed with the bellpull betwixt the bedstead and the wall. He wouldn't be locked in but they didn't want their guests wandering about backstage and he was to use the chamber pot under the bed.

When he observed it sounded as if they didn't want their guests to know too much about one another, Claudine shrugged and said, "I see you've rid the owlhoot trail before. I know the rules, too. So you'll get no argument if you want to fuck me. But please don't grab me and throw me down without warning. I ain't been a whore long and it takes some getting used to."

He said he'd try to remember that and asked how come

she'd become a whore if she had such delicate feelings.

Claudine shrugged and said, "I had no choice. My husband had no head for figures and wound up owing Mr. Shrike more than he could ever pay. So Mr. Shrike foreclosed on me."

Longarm whistled softly and asked, "Your man put his own wife up as security on a loan?"

She shrugged and replied with a gallant, defeated smile, "I was the only asset he had left. I don't cry about it no more. I'd as soon be fucked by *men* as a weakling who could neither win at cards nor quit."

She left before Longarm could observe he'd heard *that* story before. Nobody could really be named Shrike, or butcher bird. But it seemed an apt nickname for a moneylending cuss the folk in a dinky trail town had to turn to. The exact organization of the clique running Animas Point was less important than the simple fact a clique was running it, raw as hell. Flim-flamming outside lawmen with haunted whorehouses had to be rated as malicious mischief. Maintaining a wayside inn for outlaws along a deliberately spooky outlaw trail was against the law for certain, as was forcing women into prostitution.

Unless, of course, old Claudine had been ordered to test him with a sob story. He'd find out later whether he was supposed to help her escape or not. They doubtless felt they were big-city-slick, but he was beginning to suspect they might be overconfident. A master criminal was a contradiction in terms. A small town sharpy with the jingle to loan and foreclose on opera houses, whorehouses and gambler's wives should have been smart enough to see a man who owned his own town would have been better off running it at an honest, slower-but-surer rate. With the depression of the '70s over and things commencing to boom out this way again, a *really* smart crook would be studying on how to mend his ways.

As he shut the door to piss in the sink, Longarm con-

171

sidered how a money lender named for a bird that preyed on other birds might feel he was in too deep, what with the town law corrupt from top to doubtless bottom. But as the old song said, farther along he'd know more about it, and, meanwhile, he hadn't et since he'd arrived back in town.

He smoked a cheroot instead. Then Claudine came back up with a tray of coffee, cake and grub. The blue plate special he recognized from that restaurant near the hotel was roast beef, mashed potatoes and okra, that evening. The cake was marble. The coffee was Arbuckle brand. When Claudine said she'd come back later for the chinaware she warned him she never fucked as she was gathering all the trays. He asked her if she could get him something to read if he paid her for whatever she could find in the way of recent newspapers, the *Police Gazette*, mayhaps *Scientific American*.

She said she'd try. He knew she'd be carrying the trays back to the restaurant and there was a newsstand in the hotel lobby.

But before Claudine came back for Longarm's tray, Stubby Croft arrived with Longarm's money order from Denver, made out, of course, to Buck Crawford. When the town law offered to help him cash it at the one bank in town, Longarm asked, "At this hour?"

The older man who lived there said, "They'll open up for me. I'm the law. Let's go, I'll explain along the way, and vouch for your ID once we get there."

So they went down the backstairs and out the stage door as the sun stood low in the west and the supper bells had cleared the main street of Animas Point of all but a few lost souls.

They entered the bank fronting on Main Street via another alleyway side door. The portly gent waiting inside didn't ask questions. He just read the money order and took a roll from his frock coat to peel off the hundred dollars in paper. Longarm never got to examine the bills one seldom saw west of the Missouri. Stubby Croft grabbed them and put them in his pants, saying, "Let's get on back before Main Street wakes up for the evening, Buck. You're paid up for the week, now."

Longarm waited until they were alone outside before he quietly asked, "How come? Wouldn't you say a hundred dollars would be good for ten days at ten dollars a day, Stubby?"

The town law nodded agreeably and said, "It would. But your room and board just went up. We know who that was you shot in the saloon, now. He was a famous bounty hunter, and you still beat him to the draw. So fess up, Buck. You run off from that hearing at Fort Defiance on an army mule lest it come out at the trial you were somebody other than the honest and upright guide they'd hired, right?"

Longarm smiled sheepishly and replied, "If you're so smart, who do you suspect I might be?"

Stubby Croft laughed smugly and said, "Don't matter beans, as long as you can pay a hundred a week for as long as you want to stay."

Longarm asked, "What if I wanted to ride on tonight? Would I get any money back?"

Stubby told him not to talk nonsense and they parted, friendly or not, at the stage door of the opera house.

The next seventy-two hours seemed to last a million years in spite of the periodicals Claudine fetched him, asking how he could read such big words. He confessed he *couldn't* fathom each and every word in the science and travel magazines, but explained you never learned much if you stuck to what you already knew. She said she'd never met a body for so much reading without no fucking since she'd been put to work there by M. Shrike.

When she failed to say she'd do anything, anything, if only he would help her escape, Longarm began to believe

Claudine's simple sordid tale of small town knavery. Tight cliques running small towns could get brazen as all get-out, kissing each other's asses for being so all fired clever.

It was on a Thursday night, just after Claudine had cleared away his supper tray, when she came back to tell him she had to lock all the guests in for the night but offered to lock herself in with him if he wanted.

Longarm smiled down at her to reply, "I fear that dose I warned you about ain't quite cleared up, yet. But I thank you for the flattering offer, Miss Claudine. How come they want all us children locked up in our rooms tonight?"

She replied without shilly-shally, "Lawmen in town. Federal marshal and four deputies. Just checked into the hotel up the way. They'll go out to the whorehouse in a while, find nothing but regular whores, and doubtless leave in the morning like everyone else. But Stubby don't want any of you guests of Mr. Shrike bumping noses with federal lawmen by accident or on purpose. So nobody is to leave the premises until further notice."

Longarm didn't argue. The daylight from the frosted glass above him having faded some, he lit the wall sconce and flopped on the bedstead with a travel magazine as she stepped outside to lock him in.

Longarm made himself read the whole magazine. It wasn't easy. He really didn't give a shit about Madeira, as a drink or as a place to visit. But he had to give his uncle Billy time to settle in for the night. There'd been no way to tell him with that thinly coded wire that the haunted whorehouse was a red herring to lure lawman away from the real action in town.

He made himself read the *Police Gazette* a second time, in case he'd missed something or old Billy and the boys would slowpoke out to the haunted whorehouse and back. The wired reference about a mess "Buck Crawford" had gotten into in Brownsville had only been meant to remind the boss of another time he'd been working undercover and been joined in the field by the marshal in the flesh.

Longarm held out until ten P.M. before he muscled the tall wardrobe under that skylight and climbed from the bedstead to reach up and unscrew the skylight from its frame with his pocketknife. Then he lifted it off its frame and slid it to one side before he dropped back down to trim the wall sconce, don his hat, jacket and six-gun, and climb back up to hoist himself over the edge to the flat roof of the the opera house.

Moving across the gravel coated tarpaper as quietly as he could, he saw half a dozen other skylights, lit from below. Since all the glass was frosted, he didn't try to find out who Claudine was really locked in with for the night. He explored along the asshole-puckering rim until, sure thing, he found the steel ladder he'd expected, leading down to that side alley.

The stage door was shut as Longarm eased past it. He chanced a few yards of Main Street, whipped around the first corner, and approached the hotel by way of the service road running behind all the buildings on his side of Main.

But when he entered the hotel by way of their service entrance, the damned night clerk told him his damned boss and the four damned deputies from Denver were over to the damned saloon instead of up in their damned rooms where he'd wanted them to be!

So, seeing there was no other way for it, Longarm worked his way close as he could manage to that big saloon doubtless owned by Mr. Shrike. Then he boldly crossed Main Street and bulled on through the batwing doors to, sure enough, spy Billy Vail and four good old boys from the Denver federal building bellied up to the bar, along with the town law, Stubby Croft.

Stubby gasped, "Damn it, Buck! You were told to . . . never mind."

Longarm replied, "You are under arrest, Marshal Croft. Evening, Marshal Vail. 'Bout time you-all got here!"

Stubby Croft made an unwise move. Before he could get himself in real trouble, Deputy Smiley whopped him across the back of his skull with a six-gun to lay him flat as a rug on the sawdust as Deputy Dutch, a more excitable young cuss, got out his own sidearm to declare he'd shoot the first regular who moved in the guts, in the nuts, between the eyes, and then he'd *kill* 'em!

So nobody moved as Billy Vail covered the crowd with his beer schooner, asking Longarm what the fuck was going on.

Longarm explained, "That one on the floor is the town law. I hope his skull ain't fractured because once he comes to, he'll be the best one to question about the minor details. Could I have a beer?"

Billy Vail signalled the barkeep, who didn't seem about to argue. So as they sipped suds together with their pals covering the crowd, Longarm brought his boss up-to-date and added, "The others may be scattering, even as we speak. But old Stubby, there, and others I've got pegged for certain will no doubt be proud to tell us all about a small-time aiding-and-abetting operation we just busted up. Town law is appointed by the town's administration. I just cashed a money order you sent across state lines at the bank I suspect of owning most if not all of the town, including that whorehouse haunted by spooks made up with leftover opera house shit. So that's about the size of it. I don't have any hanging charges to lever any of 'em with, but I'm sure the lesser lights will turn state's evidence against our mysterious M. Shrike, a penny-ante buzzard preying on a town in trouble, for reduced sentences."

Vail scowled down at the unconscious town law to demand, "What are you talking about? Didn't you wire us days ago you'd had a shoot-out in that innocent whore-house run by penny-ante crooks?"

Longarm nodded and said, "Had another shoot-out in this very same saloon more recent. Couldn't wire you about that one. But now that I have seen the light, I can tell you true Mr. Shrike and these other pathetic shits had nothing to do with them two attempts on my life."

"Now this," Billy Vail declareed, "Is starting to get interesting!"

Chapter 20

It took but another forty-eight hours for the Denver team to get a good grip on the mess in New Mexico Territory. They wired the county sheriff's department for some help, and he sent them down a posse to assist in their roundup. Everyone at the opera house but Pops and two wanted outlaws had lit out right after Stubby's arrest, and Longarm had no call to describe the pathetic Claudine in detail.

Once Arizona was in on the all-points, Mr. Shrike, whose real handle was more like Banker Shreveport, was picked up in Tombstone by their amiable Marshal White as he was boarding the Bisbee stage with a valise filled with double eagles, doubtless bound for Old Mexico. San Juan County, New Mexico Territory, was proud to pick up all the taxable property he'd held deeds on, back when he'd still been a free man. So Longarm and his Colorado pals were free to go back to Denver as New Mexico tidied up after them, and they did so.

Forty-eight hours after that, as Longarm reported for work as usual at the federal building, late, he was intercepted in the marble halls by Portia Parkhurst Esquire, Attorney at Law, in spite of her handsome figure under the severe black outfit she wore around city, state or federal courtrooms.

As Longarm ticked his hat brim to the severely beautiful brunette who let a little premature silver show to give her an air of judicial know-how, Portia said, "Custis, I've been retained by the Hawker Mineral Trust. I'd like to talk to you about that federal warrant you swore out on one Dudly Snopes, a company detective?"

Longarm took her by one elbow to steer her toward a sort of . . . conference room down the hall as he replied, "You mean you want to talk to me about that private eye retained to track down and bring home a bratty daughter of the Hawker family?"

That had been a statement, not a question. So Portia said, "Have it your way. Call her anything you like, and you'll have barely rounded first base. But her far nicer folk have her under better control these days in a firmly run finishing school where she can't get at married men, and there's an outside chance she just might settle down to a more cautious harlot by the time they lose their control over her as legal guardians. So, really, Custis, do we have to drag Susan Hawker's name past Judge Dickerson down the hall? You know I'll just get Detective Snopes off on the merits of your ridiculous charges."

Longarm led her into an officially out-of-use and locked-up storeroom as he told her, "Ain't nothing ridiculous about not one but two attempts to assassinate a federal official. Namely me. I've probable cause to charge Detective Snopes with recruiting a hired gun called Farnsworth to say he was a Texas Ranger named Moran and tag along with me to make more than one attempt, himself. Process of eliminating. He was on guard, and I was supposed to be in a pup tent only a member of our party could be sure about when he blazed away with his own pistol and a cheap spare he'd brought along, yelling all the while to make it sound like he was on our side. Then he lobbed the gun nobody knew he owned out in the chaparral to be found by a sharp-eyed Indian, who never spotted any other sign. So I was suspicious of *him*, wondering how anybody could be trailing a mounted party across semibare range without leaving sign an Indian from a deer-hunting nation could read, when he made a fatal slip in a haunted whorehouse and knew he had to draw or explain a heap that couldn't be explained!"

As they sat down on the leather chesterfield to converse more intimate, Portia trilled, "Haunted *whorehouse*? I might have known you'd wind up in a place like that with a hired gun out to murder you!"

Longarm draped an arm along the back of the chesterfield lest she feel he was being cool to her as he explained, "Red herring, drug across an outlaw trail by another bunch. Let's stick to your client's hired help, and the hired guns he recruited to help him. I don't like to brag, but they will print yarns about me in the papers, and Snopes must have thought the fake ranger might need a backup. He was right. But that second bounty hunter, the late Roger Ford, they told me down New Mexico way, snooped around asking questions about me in Durango, then lost track of me entire when our Indian guide led us off the beaten track Ford thought he was following us along. When he lost us, he rode back to Animas Point, wired Denver for further instructions, and there he was, still waiting for me to get *back* from Fort Defiance when I walked in the door and he lost."

When he drew her closer to nuzzle her shell-like ear, Portia said, "Hold that thought, Custis. You've yet to fib to me about other *men*, so I'll buy you being beset by hired guns. That seems to happen to you a lot. But what evidence do you have that my client's glorified baby-sitter hired even one of those men to kill you?"

He nibbled her ear anyway and murmured, "Motive. A puffed-up small town money lender had plenty of reason to worry about me. I caught him, and now he's on his way to prison, too. He'll be standing trial down yonder. But nobody down yonder knew who I was until it was too late. They were hiding me out, not out to shoot me. So I knew somebody else had hired those old boys to gun me, and the private detective I met up with in an alley as he was loading Miss Susan Hawker in his shay was, and is, the only suspect who makes a lick of sense."

Portia didn't move his free hand from her lap. She patted it, as fondly as usual, even as she chided, "Custis, really, you saw Detective Snopes performing the job he'd been hired for. It wasn't supposed to be in the papers, and so it was never in the papers that the naughty, naughty Susan Hawker had been abducted from a love nest and carried home to her worried parents. Do you seriously think the Hawkers would pay to have you killed, as anxious as they might be to avoid scandal?"

Longarm began to inch her black skirts up as he replied, "Nope. I know neither the wayward girl nor her folk knew why Dudly Snopes on his own was anxious to have me killed. I ain't just guessing, honey. I asked questions around town as soon as we got back. Questions old Dudly had been afraid I might ask before he recruited those killers to prevent my asking."

Portia pleaded, "Damnit, Custis, stop feeling me up and tell me what you found out! What could Detective Snopes have feared you were liable to ask about?"

"How he got that kicking and screaming underaged spitfire out of that love nest she'd been sharing with a married man, of course. He didn't want me nor anyone else to ask where Miss Susan Hawker's married lover was, all the time she was being rescued from a life of shame and fun!"

Portia shoved his hand away to protest, "We'll talk about fun later, damnit! Are you saying Detective Snopes did something bad to Susan's child molester and the girl never *mentioned* it once Snopes got her home?"

Longarm shook his head and said, "Since she never, she never knew. The foolish older man she'd likely made the first moves on never came home from work the night before Dudly Snopes busted in to carry the doubtless worried and wondering Susan home. The man's name was Keller. Joseph Keller. He was in ladies notions when Susan Hawker got a notion to shack up with him. Whether Snopes is willing to tell us or not, it is only a question of time, once we know a man's missing, to find out where his killer buried the body. But I don't have to prove Snopes murdered anybody. I got him cold on trying to murder me. It ain't true it's *impossible* to get copies of telegrams from Western Union, given a federal court order."

Portia stared wild-eyed at Longarm to marvel, "God, *damn* you're good, and I'm not just talking about bedtime! But how are we to leave Susan and her parents out if I persuade him to surrender and throw himself upon the mercy of the court?"

Longarm shrugged and replied, "That ain't for me to say. I just arrest 'em. The prosecution and presiding judge make any deals. Do you really reckon you can persuade Snopes to come in quietly?"

She rose to her high heels, saying, "It's my job to smooth things over for my clients. I have Detective Snopes on tap right down the hall in another side chamber. I told him to wait there while I talked to you about that warrant. I mean to chide him about neglecting to inform me he was more guilty than charged. But wait here and I'll see if I can convince him confession is good for the soul and sometimes ten years off."

So Longarm stepped out in the hall with her and waited there as Portia strode mannishly off to duck into a distant doorway. Young Henry, the squirt who played the typewriter for Billy Vail, paused in flight as he was dashing along the same hall with papers to file and asked in his snotty way whether Longarm had any notion of what time it was.

Longarm said, "I'm already on duty this morning, Henry. Fixing to make an arrest before I report in to you, official."

Henry just got to ask what Longarm was talking about when they both heard the dulcet barks of muffled pistol shots. A .32-Short, from the sounds of it.

Drawing his more serious six-gun as he charged down the hall with Henry tearing after, for Henry only *looked* like a sissy, Longarm burst in on Portia Parkhurst Esquire and her client to find Detective Snopes spread-eagled on the floor, smiling up glassy-eyed at the demure lady standing over him with a smoking purse pistol in one dainty hand.

As Longarm hunkered down to feel for a pulse, Portia explained, "I had to. It was self-defense. When I accused him of attempted murder, he attempted to murder me."

Longarm removed Snopes's snub-nosed Colt from its shoulder holster to place it quietly on the marble floor near the dead man's upturned derby as he soberly replied, "Anyone can see why you had to defend yourself, Miss Portia. It's open-and-shut. Wouldn't you agree, Henry?"

Henry allowed it sure looked like self-defense to him. Henry was no fool.

So that was how the shooting of Dudly Snopes went down on paper, and since the obvious maniac who'd attacked his own lawyer in a courtroom had never mentioned Miss Susan Hawker or her family, Longarm felt no call to pursue why the same maniac had sent hired guns after *him*. Some old boys just seemed to be crazy-mean when it came to lawyers and lawmen.

It took the Denver P.D. and a bloodhound, acting on a tip from Longarm, another forty-eight hours to recover the badly decomposed and awesomely stinky remains of the late Joseph Keller.

After they'd failed to find him under the dirt floor of his shop's cellar, they'd naturally failed to find him under the carriage house he'd hired as his love nest for an underage runaway. So, following a natural process of elimination, they'd found him in the cesspit under the backyard privy behind his notions shop.

Longarm had told them the strong-arm hired by the gal's family would have done her lover in on the premises of his shop to get the key to that love nest and bust in on the kid unexpected and unhampered by a bigger man than himself.

The best way it worked for Longarm, Snopes had killed Keller around closing time, let the body lay for later, then gone to haul sassy Susan Hawker kicking and screaming to meet up in the alley with a deputy U.S. marshal he had to smooth talk, sudden.

Then, after he'd delivered the young sass to her worried parents, and likely sweating bullets all the while, Snopes had gone back to the notions shop in the wee small hours, disposed of the body, and sent for outside help to dispose of the only witness outside the family who was still alive, before anyone else could get him to establish a possible motive for the evaporation of an established downtown busineman who'd rented a carriage house nowheres near his shop or home address.

So with the help of Portia Parkhurst Esquire and the Hawker Trust, the murder of Joseph Keller was described in the local papers as a store holdup gone wrong, with no connection to the madness of Dudly Snopes, who'd set out to murder lawmen and lawyers for reasons he took with him to his grave.

Longarm was just as glad the Widow Keller would collect on her dead fool's life insurance policy, as she might not have, had the underwriters been able to prove a death by suicidal chippie-chasing.

For after the many nights in bed with the same lawyer,

the slap-and-tickle had commenced to feel like work, and he still had to tell that other gal what she'd been doing for him when she carried that wire to his dear old aunt and uncle down Sherman Street from her place.

Longarm was sort of looking forward to telling her. She and Portia were about as different as two gals could get without either of them being ugly.

Watch for

LONGARM AND THE MYSTERIOUS MISTRESS

285th novel in the exciting LONGARM series
from Jove

Coming in August!